Nate turned and backed Chelsea up a step. "I think I understand what's going on."

"You do? Mind clueing me in?" she asked.

"You're scared."

She blinked at him. "Of what?"

"Not of *what*...of *who*?" He caught her gaze and held it.

"I'm not scared of you, Nate, if that's what you're thinking," she stammered. "You've been nothing but helpful."

His smile was devastating. Good-looking was almost an insult to say about a man as hot as Nate. He had that animal magnetism she'd heard about but rarely seen. His piercing steel eyes and carved-from-granite jawline coupled with thick, curly dark hair made for one seriously hot package. The man worked out. His body was defined in places she didn't even realize there could be muscles.

"If not of me, then maybe of this." He brought his hand up to her chin and tilted her mouth toward his.

WHAT SHE DID

USA TODAY Bestselling Author

BARB HAN

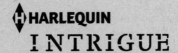

HARLEQUIN
INTRIGUE

All my love to Brandon, Jacob and Tori,
my favorite people in the world.

To Babe, my hero, for being my great love and
my place to call home.

To my mom, Juanita, for being my biggest cheerleader. And to my
sister, Tonia, for always having my back. Love you both!

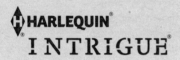

ISBN-13: 978-1-335-13641-1

What She Did

Copyright © 2020 by Barb Han

All rights reserved. No part of this book may be used or reproduced in
any manner whatsoever without written permission except in the case of
brief quotations embodied in critical articles and reviews.

This is a work of fiction. Names, characters, places and incidents
are either the product of the author's imagination or are used fictitiously.
Any resemblance to actual persons, living or dead, businesses,
companies, events or locales is entirely coincidental.

This edition published by arrangement with Harlequin Books S.A.

For questions and comments about the quality of this book,
please contact us at CustomerService@Harlequin.com.

Harlequin Enterprises ULC
22 Adelaide St. West, 40th Floor
Toronto, Ontario M5H 4E3, Canada
www.Harlequin.com

Printed in U.S.A.

Recycling programs
for this product may
not exist in your area.

PLEASE RECYCLE
THIS PRODUCT IS RECYCLABLE

USA TODAY bestselling author **Barb Han** lives in north Texas with her very own hero-worthy husband, three beautiful children, a spunky golden retriever/standard poodle mix and too many books in her to-read pile. In her downtime, she plays video games and spends much of her time on or around a basketball court. She loves interacting with readers and is grateful for their support. You can reach her at barbhan.com.

Books by Barb Han

Harlequin Intrigue

Rushing Creek Crime Spree

Cornered at Christmas
Ransom at Christmas
Ambushed at Christmas
What She Did

Crisis: Cattle Barge

Sudden Setup
Endangered Heiress
Texas Grit
Kidnapped at Christmas
Murder and Mistletoe
Bulletproof Christmas

Cattlemen Crime Club

Stockyard Snatching
Delivering Justice
One Tough Texan
Texas-Sized Trouble
Texas Witness
Texas Showdown

Harlequin Intrigue Noir

Atomic Beauty

Visit the Author Profile page at Harlequin.com.

CAST OF CHARACTERS

Chelsea McGregor—An inheritance changes her luck. Will it make her a target?

Nate Kent—This Kent brother interferes with a criminal's plan and puts himself in the line of fire.

Skylar—Is this little girl ready for a new life?

Travis Zucker—Chelsea's ex has disappeared without a trace. Or has he been watching all along?

Renaldo Vinchesa—This former boss is fixated on Chelsea. How far will he go to get her back?

Chapter One

"Skylar, it's time to go," Chelsea McGregor shouted up the stairs to her four-year-old daughter. She listened for the sounds of those still-small bare feet running on the creaky wood flooring of the new house in Jacobstown. Skylar's energy never ceased to amaze Chelsea. The kid had two speeds: full-out and passed out. And she was being way too quiet for this hour of the morning.

Chelsea called to her daughter again.

At least they'd made it through the first night in a new house. The move to a new town in Texas, a fresh start, had been the only light of hope in Chelsea's life since the first time she'd looked into her newborn baby's eyes. In that moment of pure bliss, Chelsea had had no idea what was going on at home. Anything of value was being cleaned out of her house while both her personal and business accounts were also being drained by the man who'd promised to love and protect her for the rest of her life.

Travis Zucker had robbed her blind, cost her

her livelihood and, to be honest, her dignity. She'd been young and naïve in falling for a charmer. He'd charmed her right out of her life's work.

People talked about defining moments. That had been hers.

When Travis hadn't answered any of her texts while she was in labor, she'd gone from fearing her husband had gotten into a terrible car accident—because she'd thought there was no way he'd miss the birth of their daughter otherwise—to laboring for seventeen hours with her mother at her side, to shock followed by horror that she had a brand-new life to care for and no financial means to do it with. She and Skylar had moved in with Chelsea's mother, whose health had been declining for years. Linda McGregor had high blood pressure and cholesterol, diabetes, and arthritis to name a few. Staying on top of her medications and having the money to pay for them had been a challenge.

"Hey, Mom," Chelsea shouted up the stairs to her mother, who was helping Skylar get dressed for preschool. "How's it going up there?"

Her mother appeared at the top of the wooden banister.

"I sent her down." Linda checked her watch. "Must've been at least five minutes ago."

"That's odd. I didn't hear her." Chelsea spun around and scanned the long hallway past the boxes that had been stacked and pushed haphazardly against the wall.

She immediately checked the hall bathroom but

it was empty. Skylar might be playing a game. She loved hide-and-seek. Or she might be trying to avoid her first day at a new school.

Skylar had to be upstairs. There was only one staircase in the house. It creaked and groaned even under the weight of a child. Chelsea had already flagged a couple of random nails sticking out that would need to be addressed soon. Her to-do list was growing considering the place hadn't been updated or repaired in probably a good twenty years. None of the imperfections mattered. This house was a gift beyond measure.

"Where are you, little bit?" Chelsea tried to regulate her breathing as her stress levels climbed. She reminded herself that the man who'd taken everything from her wouldn't come back for their daughter. The fear was unrealistic. And yet it could be crippling when it struck. This was one of those moments.

Chelsea reminded herself to breathe slowly as she checked behind boxes, shivering in the drafty hall. There was a door to a small storage space underneath the stairs. It was possible that Skylar could've tiptoed downstairs and slipped inside. Chelsea had been in the kitchen making Skylar's lunch for her first day in a new school. A new month. A new house. A new lease on life.

Her mother had agreed to come live with Chelsea in Jacobstown. Chelsea had said she needed help with Skylar to convince her mother to leave Houston but the reality was that she was worried about her mother. Her health was a concern and Chelsea needed to be able to keep an eye on her. A group of doctors in Fort Worth had a great reputation and Chelsea figured a change couldn't hurt considering her mother's Houston doctors seemed to be running out of ideas and inspiration. They'd played around with her mother's medications, which had led to all kinds of side effects. Getting the balance right proved tricky.

A cold front had blown in during the night. Seventy-five-degree temperatures had dropped into the low forties.

Chelsea rubbed her arms to stave off the cold and called her daughter's name again.

Skylar didn't so much as make a peep.

Chelsea quickened her pace, knocking empty boxes out of her way as she locked her gaze onto the door underneath the stairs that had been made into a small coat closet.

"Hey, sweet girl. Are you in here?" Chelsea opened the door with her heart in her throat. Her calm words belied her panic.

There was no sign of Skylar.

Now, Chelsea was jogging through the rooms, double-checking the small powder room near the kitchen.

She returned to the bottom of the stairs and called up to her mother. "She's not down here. Are you sure she isn't upstairs with you?"

"I'll double-check her room." There was worry in her mother's voice, too.

Chelsea ran to the kitchen.

If Skylar was playing a joke, this wasn't funny anymore.

"Come on out of your hiding place." Chelsea drummed up her I'm-not-kidding tone. Her Serious Mom voice was nothing to mess with and maybe because she only used it as a last resort did it always work.

She listened for sounds of movement. When none came, her heart lurched. She stormed toward the stairs, panic slamming into her with the force of a tornado, threatening to rip her apart and smack her into the ground when it was done with her.

Chelsea broke into a run and by the time she hit the stairs her body was already trembling. She took the wooden steps two at a clip and then sprinted toward her daughter's bedroom.

What was it about her life that caused the walls to come tumbling down around her just when everything seemed to be clicking?

"Skylar," she said so loudly it startled her mother.

"I can't find her." Linda squinted her eyes as her right hand went over her heart; habitual signs that she was out of options. It was also the expression she'd worn the few times Chelsea had asked about her own father.

At a young age, Chelsea had realized the topic brought painful memories to her mother. She'd since learned not to ask.

Once, her mother had asked twelve-year-old Chelsea to run and get muscle strain cream from her nightstand. When Chelsea had picked it up, accidentally knocking a book to the floor, a photograph had fallen out. The picture had been a younger version of her mother. Although, to be honest, Chelsea had barely recognized the woman with the carefree smile. She'd traced the beaming face with her index finger. Gone were the deep worry grooves from her forehead—a now-hardened face from years spent barely getting by on odd jobs. Her mother had had to sacrifice going to college to support Chelsea's father, whom she later found out had been an aspiring photographer. She'd made the connection years afterward that he had taken the picture of her mother.

Money had always been tight and Chelsea often wondered what had happened to her father. There'd been times when Chelsea and her mother had had to pick up in the middle of the night and leave all their belongings behind to avoid being forced out because her mother couldn't pay the rent.

The two of them had bounced around among well-meaning relatives for most of Chelsea's life. Chelsea had picked up on late-night conversations. Her father had gone out for milk and never returned.

She'd learned that in those first couple of years after her own father left that her mother believed he'd been injured somewhere and was unable to come home. And then, as time went on, she'd hear about a relative who'd seen her husband and then another sighting from a friend of a friend. Over time, her mother seemed to realize that he'd made the choice to leave. No explanation. No looking back.

Travis had been nothing more than history repeating itself. When he'd walked out, Chelsea had no such fantasies that he'd return. She'd accepted her fate and moved on.

She thought about Travis and the similarities. Unlike her mother, Chelsea had never searched for her husband.

The worst part for Chelsea during her childhood had been seeing the hope in her mother's eyes while on road trips—trips she later realized were voyages to locate Chelsea's father. Her mother would come alive for a few days. She'd stay up late and talk until Chelsea's eyelids grew so heavy they closed automatically. She'd splurge on eating at a restaurant, which Chelsea now realized was nothing more than a truck stop but had felt like five-star dining to a kid.

Before the day ended, her mother would produce a chocolate bar. The two would curl up in a motel room bed and break off piece after piece until it had disappeared. Looking back, Chelsea had also realized that every road trip she'd taken with her mother had ended at a photography exhibit.

At least one of her aunts had believed that her father had changed his name and was living in New York. A trip there at fifteen years old had amounted to a hot, sticky bus ride and a whole heap of disappointment. Her mother had quietly cried after she'd believed Chelsea had gone to sleep, just like all the other times.

Chelsea had started a successful food truck at nineteen and within two years owned three. She'd been so proud of her business, of her ability to financially support a mother who had given up everything to care for her only daughter. She'd met Travis two years later and married after a whirlwind romance because she'd found out she was pregnant despite taking birth control pills.

To have everything she'd worked for taken away was a hot poker in Chelsea's chest.

The thought of anything happening to her daughter was worse.

"Where could she have gone?" Linda threw her hands in the air, exacerbated.

"Maybe she slipped outside and is waiting in the car." Chelsea couldn't let herself think the worst.

She hurried to the front window so she could see her used pickup truck. She'd bought it with some of the small—but enormous in so many ways—inheritance money. Since losing her business four years ago, she'd gone to work in Renaldo Vinchesa's kitchen as a sous chef. It was pretty much the only job she could get after losing everything. He was notorious for being a womanizer despite being married with kids, something she didn't learn until she'd been on the job a few weeks. She'd rejected his advances, which seemed to make him even more determined to pursue her. He'd promised to leave his wife if Chelsea agreed to go out with him—an offer that had turned her stomach.

And then, when his wife left him, he seemed to turn up the heat, pressuring Chelsea to date him or risk him smearing her reputation in the food service industry.

Vinchesa was powerful in the Houston culinary scene and his threats to ensure she'd never work in another restaurant weren't idle. He'd deliver on them in a heartbeat and, based on the texts she'd received from the couple of friends she'd made while working at Chez Houston, wheels were already turning in that direction.

Vinchesa had tried to corner her into staying put when she'd turned in her notice. Her aunt's inheritance had freed her. So she didn't mind a creaky old house, because it was *hers*. She didn't mind the elbow grease it would need to become ship-shape, because it would provide a home base for Skylar to grow up secure in. And she didn't mind that the heater had conked out in the middle of the night, because... Well, admittedly, that part had been awful.

What she did mind was her daughter pulling a Houdini.

Glancing down at the late-model pickup she'd bought, Skylar was nowhere to be seen.

"Where's my cell?" Chelsea's pockets were empty. Had she left it on the kitchen counter?

"I'll keep looking up here. You go down and check there," Linda said.

Chelsea turned to head toward the kitchen as her mother continued her closet inspection, picking up empty boxes and shaking them as though Skylar might tumble out of one.

A moment of I-can't-do-this struck. Chelsea hammered it down. She *could* do anything she wanted. She *would* pull on her big-girl pants and keep it together.

As she wheeled down the stairs and past the front door, the silhouette of a male figure appeared on the porch.

Funny, she hadn't seen anyone drive up, but then the house sat close to the road and she couldn't hear much over the howling winds picking up speed by the minute.

Heartbeat pounding at the base of her throat, she froze.

Three rapid knocks sounded at the door, followed by a masculine voice that sent warm vibrations rippling through her despite the frigid temperature.

A couple of thoughts raced through Chelsea's mind at that moment. She quickly crossed off the first. *That* voice did not belong to Renaldo. His was like fingernails on a chalkboard.

The other had to do with Skylar missing.

Chelsea bolted to the door and whisked it open.

Six foot three of male muscle under a gray cowboy hat stood on her porch. He looked to be in his early thirties with steel eyes and what she imagined would be a six-pack of pure power beneath his lightweight shirt.

The wind almost forced the door out of her hands but she held tight.

"My name's Nathan Kent and someone in this residence called in a fire." He examined her and then looked right past her. His voice would make reading a medicine bottle sound scandalous.

"A what?" Chelsea tried to ignore the inappropriate reaction her body had to the tall, gorgeous cowboy. She was confused because her cell was nowhere to be found and her mother hadn't made that call—

And then it dawned on her.

"Mom, she's okay," Chelsea called upstairs before turning back to the fireman. "Who called you?"

"A little girl by the name of Skylar was all Dispatch could get from her. A truck is on the way. I happened to be passing by when the call came in."

"I'm so sorry," she said, spinning around to check the hallway in case the little culprit stood behind her. Relief flooded her that her daughter was okay. Skylar was a good kid, just scared, and she'd just learned how to call 9-1-1 at her old school when a fireman had come to visit her class. "My daughter's starting a new school today and we just moved in to a new house, and, as you can see, there's nothing on fire here." Chelsea motioned around awkwardly, not especially sure what to do with her hands. "I'm embarrassed that she wasted your time."

Nathan made a quick call to the Dispatcher, relaying the news this was a false alarm before tucking the phone in his front pocket. Chelsea expected him to pull out a citation book and write her a ticket or something.

Instead his intense expression softened when he asked, "Mind if I speak to the caller before I go?"

"She might not come out," Chelsea said. "I'm

pretty sure she knows that she's in big trouble."
Chelsea emphasized the last two words to make
sure that Skylar heard them.

This probably wasn't the time to think about the
fact that she hadn't brushed her hair yet or that she
was wearing baggy sweatpants and a faded Journey
concert T-shirt she'd bought from a resale shop because she liked the music and the shirt fit into her
barely existent clothing budget.

Chelsea also didn't want to think about the fact
that it felt like history repeating itself with her financial situation, too. She'd sworn never to let Skylar
know what it was like to go without. At this point,
Chelsea hadn't exactly broken the promise to her
four-and-a-half-year-old daughter.

Liar, a little voice in her head accused her.

"Would you like to come in, Nathan?" Chelsea asked. If embarrassment could kill a person,
she'd be flat on the floor by now. And she sincerely
hoped the handsome cowboy/fireman believed the
red flush to her cheeks, as she felt them flame even
more when he stepped inside, was attributed to her
reaction to the situation and not to the very real attraction she felt.

"Call me Nate," he said.

Chelsea chalked her reaction up to not having had
time for a date in months. Her mother had become
sicker in recent months, and working full-time while
caring for a preschooler and aging mother left very
little social time. Not to mention the fact that the last
date she'd gone on had been such a dud that Chel-

sea had tried to convince herself she could swear off men until Skylar was eighteen. Fourteen years to go and she was already practically drooling over the first hot guy. Well played, Chelsea.

"The fireman's here, Skylar. I know you called. Mommy's worried and I want you to come out from wherever you're hiding right now." Chelsea softened her tone because, first and foremost, she was relieved her daughter was okay. Now that she knew Skylar was hiding and not stuck somewhere she couldn't call out for help, Chelsea relaxed below panic as she forced the door closed against the strong winds.

Nate stood in the front hall and Chelsea realized how bad her manners were.

"Can I get you something? A cup of coffee?" She looked him up and down. He wore jeans and a cotton shirt. The material on both was thin. He had to be cold.

He nodded. "Coffee, if it's not too much trouble."

"Follow me." She walked into the kitchen trying to think. "I know exactly where she'd be in our old house."

The hot cowboy leaned his hip against the counter and her heart stuttered when she thought about such a good-looking man standing in her kitchen.

He pulled his cell from his pocket and she noticed how graceful his movements were. He seemed like the type who would probably laugh at hearing himself described in that manner. Chelsea poured two cups of fresh brew and handed one over.

"What's your number?" he asked.

Her immediate reaction was to tense up.

He blinked at her like he was confused by her response. And then it must've dawned on him because he lowered his voice to church-quiet and said, "We'll hear it ring. But, if you're not comfortable—"

"It's okay." She whispered her number to him. This was turning out to be a red-letter day and Chelsea hadn't finished her first cup of coffee yet.

"My mother's upstairs. In fact, I'm surprised she hasn't been down here to check on things. I hope she heard me. She's most likely still looking for Skylar." The house wasn't that big. Had her mother had another episode? Chelsea's imagination was running away with her because Mother would've hollered if anything had happened. Chelsea excused herself and walked down the hall to the bottom of the stairs again, grabbing onto the wood railing that needed a few nails to steady it.

"Mom, can you listen for my ringtones?" she shouted upstairs.

"Who was at the door?" her mother asked, appearing at the landing and scaring the hell out of Chelsea. Thankfully, her mother looked normal.

"Fireman," she responded and, before her mother could freak out, added, "Everything's fine."

"I'll keep an ear open," Linda said, giving a thumbs-up sign.

Chelsea hoped her mother was making the gesture because she caught onto the plan and not because she thought Chelsea should flirt with their guest. When Mom winked, it was pretty obvious which side she was on.

Hot cowboy or no, Chelsea couldn't be bothered with so much riding on her business getting off the ground. There was a lot of work to be done and she needed to focus on making sure the three of them didn't starve.

Plus, her immediate need was to find her daughter. Nothing overrode that.

Nate Kent entered the hallway and Chelsea didn't have to look to know he was there. She could feel his masculine presence. She turned and him gave the awkward hand signal her mother had just given her, with an even cheesier smile.

Chelsea took a breath and fisted her hand.

He seemed to get the idea because he tapped the call button.

A hush seemed to fall over the house and even the roaring winds outside calmed.

Chelsea listened, moving from room to room when no ringtones sounded. Her daughter was too young to change the settings on the phone. This couldn't be right. Skylar was hiding somewhere. She'd called 9-1-1 and asked for help.

The cowboy followed her until they ended up back in the kitchen.

"It's gone into voice mail."

Chapter Two

The look of terror on the brown-eyed, blond-haired mother punched Nate in the gut. The five-and-a-half-foot tall beauty had full lips, creamy skin and a flawless figure with just the right amount of curves. And those were things Nate had no business noticing.

"If she was okay, she would answer." Chelsea twisted her fingers together.

An older woman wearing a frock and apron came into the kitchen. "Any luck down here?"

"No." Chelsea looked frantic as she exited the kitchen and moved from room to room calling for her daughter.

"I'm Linda," the older woman said. She had permanent worry lines etched into her forehead and sad, light brown eyes. Maybe sad wasn't the right word. Deep down, behind her smile, she looked empty. She was thick around the middle and it looked like it took some effort to walk. But there was also a kindness and warmth to her that her daughter had no doubt inherited.

"Pleasure to meet you, ma'am. Name's Nate Kent." He offered a handshake that she took with a surprising amount of vigor for a woman of her stature.

His cell buzzed. He excused himself as he checked the screen and saw the call was from Dispatch.

"Are you still at the McGregor residence?" Patty Smart had turned seventy-eight on her last birthday and her mind was still sharp as a tack.

"Yes, ma'am."

"Good. I have a little girl on the line and she's quite distraught. Seems she's gotten herself in a fix." Patty's calm, sympathetic voice was a welcome relief. It meant the little girl was okay.

"Is she in the house?" He shot a knowing look toward Chelsea. Even wearing baggy jogging pants and a loose T-shirt, he could tell she had an amazing figure. Again, her shapely hips and full breasts were none of his business.

"Yes. She's in a closet under the stairwell," Patty supplied.

"We looked inside there." Nate was already circling back with Chelsea on his heels.

"Can you hold on, please?" Patty asked.

"Of course." Nate turned to Chelsea and whispered, "She called 9-1-1. I'm on the phone with one of the operators. Your daughter's here in the house and she's shaken up but all right." Nate was grateful he could deliver good news. As a volunteer fireman for Broward County, he'd seen a little bit of everything and not every situation turned out the way he'd like.

"Thank you." Chelsea's eyes closed for a second and she looked to be collecting herself as relief washed over her features. "If she's here, where is she?"

He nodded at the hall closet as Patty came back on the line.

Chelsea's forehead creased with confusion.

There could be a crawl space in there. He'd seen plenty of oddities in these old houses. People created insulated spaces to hide money and, in some cases, bootleg whiskey.

"I'm putting the call on speaker," Nate said to Patty.

"Skylar said she's worried that her mommy is going to get upset with her for being bad. She didn't want to start a new school." Patty's grandmotherly compassion came through.

"She's safe. That's all that matters to me," Chelsea said.

"I'm sorry it took a minute to call. You must be worried sick. It took time to calm her down enough to understand what she was saying."

Chelsea was already inside the four-by-six closet with its sloped ceiling.

Nate peeked inside.

"She's not in here." Chelsea dropped to all fours and felt around on the floor.

"None of these houses have basements." Nate had

no idea where the blond beauty had moved from. This was Old Lady Barstock's place.

Chelsea felt around walls. "There's nothing here."

"Can you tell Skylar to shout to us or bang on the wall?" Nate dropped to all fours and knocked on the walls, looking for a dead space.

And then he felt it. A ridge where there should have been solid wall. "Hold on. I might have something."

He ran his finger along the ridge. Chelsea moved beside him and her scent washed over him. She had that clean, warm and citrusy smell.

Refocusing, Nate pushed on the two-by-two box. The wall moved. Using both hands, he forced an opening. Almost instantly, sniffles sounded.

"Skylar, baby, are you in there?" Chelsea's voice had a forced calm that belied the wild look in her eyes.

"Momma?" A sob echoed as a scuffling movement sounded. The little girl's face appeared in the opening, round and angelic. Red, puffy eyes spilled tears when she saw her mother.

Nate backed away, ending the call with Patty after delivering the good news, giving mother and daughter space to reunite.

Linda paced in the hallway. "Was that her voice I heard?"

"She's okay."

The older woman clutched at her chest and it looked like her right knee gave out. Nate grabbed her arm to keep her from falling.

"Let's get you into a comfortable chair." He helped Linda into the kitchen and into a chair at the table.

Linda apologized several times.

"Don't worry about it. Happens all the time." It didn't, but he wanted to make her feel better. The family had clearly been through enough for one morning.

Nate didn't have children of his own but a few of his brothers did. He couldn't imagine the terror of one going missing even for a few minutes.

His family had been through a lot and that had made them even closer.

Their parents had died a short time apart, leaving Nate, his four brothers and one sister to run the family ranch. The Kent Ranch, known to most simply as KR, was one of the most successful cattle ranches in Texas. The family owned land across the state and into Idaho and Wyoming.

Then there was the growing problem of someone butchering heifers on the family ranch. The gruesome killings had started out weeks ago with one heifer found near Rushing Creek with its left hoof hacked off before being left to die. There was no excuse for animal cruelty to any Kent, and Nate was no exception. His family had been working closely with local Sheriff Zach McWilliams, who was also a relative, to solve the cases. The cousins had been close from childhood, along with Zach's sister, Amy.

Everyone was on the hunt. There had been no new information or leads on the case yet extra patrols couldn't keep the killer at bay. His pattern of striking was unpredictable.

"I don't want to be any trouble," Linda said, settling in the chair.

"You couldn't be," Nate reassured her. He had basic EMT training but that's about as far as his skills went.

Linda's color had washed out, her pupils dilated.

"Are you taking any medications?" he asked.

The older woman issued a breath. "I forgot. In all the excitement, I completely missed my morning pills."

Chelsea came into the room, a little girl in her arms who looked like her Mini-Me but with black, kinky curls. Nate glanced up and his heart squeezed at the sight of mother and daughter. The little girl was still sniffling and softly crying, her face buried in her mother's long hair.

Linda put up a hand at Chelsea's obvious concern. "I forgot to take my medication this morning," Linda said.

"Where is it? I'll go get it." Chelsea was busy with her little girl, so Nate volunteered to do it.

"I keep them in the cabinet next to the kitchen sink." Linda pointed. "There's a lock on it so you'll have to finagle it open."

"A couple of my brothers are married with kids. I've seen most of these." He was able to open the cabinet easily. He grabbed three bottles with Linda's name on them and brought them to Chelsea's mother with a glass of water. He recognized one as a commonly prescribed blood pressure medication.

She thanked him and took the offering. She opened the bottles and popped three pills in her mouth. "I'll be back to normal in no time."

Nate noticed the concern on Chelsea's forehead. She had her hands full.

And so did he.

"THANK YOU FOR COMING," Chelsea said to Nate. Her to-do list was piling up and she hadn't planned on Skylar being around for the day. Having her daughter home was going to throw a wrench in things. Part of her figured she should send her daughter to preschool, but the other part—the winning part—convinced her to keep Skylar home.

What Skylar had done was not okay. But the scare of being locked inside the crawl space had been bad enough for her daughter to still cling to Chelsea. There'd be no peeling those fingers from around Chelsea's neck, and maybe she was a bad parent for it, but she needed to keep eyes on her little girl after that shock, to see that her daughter was fine.

Chelsea, shaken up by the morning's events, was probably overreacting, but she also acknowledged that she'd uprooted Skylar from everything familiar.

Nate finished his cup of coffee and set it on the counter.

"There's no reason to rush him out the door," Linda said with a little wink that made Chelsea's face flame with embarrassment.

Worse yet, he chuckled, and it was a rumble from deep in his chest.

"I'll walk you out." Chelsea didn't care how amused he was. She was mortified.

"Hope you feel better soon," he said to her mother.

"Maybe you could stop in later."

"Mom."

Chelsea, Skylar in her arms, led the way to the front door without looking back. She didn't want to give away her body's reaction to the handsome cowboy. Besides, it was most likely because of what had happened, but she had a creepy feeling that she couldn't shake. When she really thought about it, she'd woken with it.

A premonition? She didn't believe in psychic abilities.

She stopped at the door, hefting Skylar higher on her hip. "I think I've apologized like fifty times already, but I'm sorry about my mother just now."

"She was having a little fun." She was grateful for his good nature. He hesitated at the door. "I don't want to intrude, but it might be safer if I check out that crawl space before I leave."

Skylar lifted her head to look up. She'd always been a shy child, avoiding eye contact until it was absolutely necessary.

"It was scary," Skylar said, brown eyes wide and watery. A tear escaped, rolling down her cheek. She brought the back of her hand up to wipe it away.

Chelsea almost didn't know how to react. Her

daughter rarely spoke to strangers, especially men she didn't know.

Nate's offer would take an item off Chelsea's growing to-do list. Accepting help was foreign to her, especially from a stranger. She had always been self-reliant. To be honest, she preferred it to depending on anyone else.

But she could also admit that she was in over her head.

"That would be great." She needed to get back to the kitchen to check on her mother, though she didn't like the idea of the crawl space being open. "Any chance you can board it up while you're here? I have a hammer and nails. I'm sure I can find a couple of boards."

"I was going to offer the same thing. Thought I'd check it out first to make sure nothing else was in there."

Chelsea must've tensed without realizing.

"In case there are any small critters in there that need to get out first," he clarified.

She wasn't sure she loved the sound of that, either, but it was a nice gesture. Being in the country would take some getting used to. "You must love animals." Wasn't his last name Kent?

He nodded and smiled. Those gray eyes of his shouldn't make her feel like her knees might buckle when he looked at her.

He was just a man. Okay, that wasn't entirely fair. He was more than a man. He was one seriously gorgeous cowboy with a familiar last name—why did she know it?

"You could say taking care of animals is in my blood."

"Do you have any?" Skylar asked, perking up.

"I live on a ranch where there are cattle, horses and pretty much every other wild thing you can find in Texas." Normally a man of his size and build would be intimidating to a small child. His gentle nature with Skylar made it easy to see why her daughter took to him.

Chelsea glanced at his ring finger and her heart gave a little flip when she didn't see a gold band. Not that it mattered, she quickly reminded herself.

Skylar's face lit up as the cowboy spoke. She leaned away from her mother and unclenched her hands from around her mother's neck. She rocked her body, indicating that she wanted to get down. Chelsea complied.

Her daughter had never recovered from a traumatic event so fast. Chelsea's head was spinning and she knew better than to look a gift horse in the mouth.

"Do you have a pony?" Skylar asked.

"We have three. Peter, Polka and Dot," he supplied much to Skylar's amusement. "Peter bites, so you have to watch out for him if you ever stop by."

"Can I come over now?" Skylar twisted her arms together and shifted from foot to foot.

"No, honey. Mr. Kent is working and you should be at your first day of school. Remember?" Chelsea couldn't help herself but to throw in that last part. Now that her own heart rate had settled below panic she was rethinking her position on keeping Sky home. If there was a chance she could get her daughter to school, even late, she probably should do it. Having even a few hours to focus would go a long way toward getting her restaurant ready for its opening in six weeks. *Six weeks?* Thinking about it made her lungs squeeze.

"What school do you go to?" Nate asked, squatting until he was eye level with the child.

Skylar looked up at her mother and blinked.

"Clemens Preschool. Have you heard of it?" It was an early childhood development program and the best part was that tuition was next to nothing— precisely what Chelsea could afford while she got her business off the ground.

"I know a few of the teachers over there. Mrs. Eaton—"

Skylar jump-clapped, which was quite a sight, considering she'd never jumped and clapped at the same time before. "That's my teacher's name." Skylar could barely contain her excitement.

Shock nearly knocked Chelsea back a step. Skylar's reaction had caught Chelsea off guard but then she'd never seen Skylar react to a man this way. Her little girl had never met her own father and there'd been no grandfather around to fill in the gap.

Chelsea's attempt to sign her daughter up for a coed soccer team had fallen flat when Skylar had refused to step on the pitch. In her daughter's defense, the coach had had a supersonic voice that boomed. He was Dad to seven boisterous boys and coached middle school football. He was big, round and loud. Skylar had been terrified of him.

"Your teacher brings in a special visitor every year around this time," Nate said. "A male frog by the name of Henry."

"Really?" Skylar's eyes were saucers. She was captivated. Her mother could admit to being enthralled by the handsome cowboy, too. The man most likely had a girlfriend or significant other. There was no way he was single and, even if he was, Chelsea had been there, done that, and the T-shirt had been stolen by her ex.

"That's right," he said. Chelsea already knew from checking his ring finger earlier there was no band, which didn't necessarily mean there was no relationship.

Besides, once this cowboy was on his way, Chelsea planned to have a serious discussion with her daughter about the proper use of 9-1-1. Although, in fairness, the little girl had been trapped between the walls. Chelsea shivered thinking about how badly this could've gone if her daughter hadn't taken the cell phone in with her.

A cold trickle, like when people said a cat walked over their grave, crept over her. She'd been on edge for days and it was probably because of the way she'd left things at her job in Houston.

Renaldo had made threats before telling her she'd regret walking out on him. He'd been outraged at the fact that she didn't want to date him and her quitting had seemed to infuriate him more. She would've walked out after the first time he'd made a pass at her but she'd needed the job and would need a letter of recommendation if she quit. She'd been forced to keep the peace.

Looking back she could see how naïve she'd been in believing his interest would blow over. She figured he'd lose interest and find another person to date. It wasn't like many of the other waitresses didn't see him as attractive. To Chelsea, he seemed like a spoiled middle-aged man used to getting what he wanted from people. There was absolutely nothing attractive about that to her.

Renaldo had made no secret of being put off by her rebuttals.

The man had an ego the size of Texas.

But was it dangerous?

Chapter Three

Nate had picked up a sidekick while he worked. Skylar was a cute little thing with big, rust-colored eyes and a shy smile. He'd been around kids enough recently, thanks to his brothers and their wives, to be halfway decent as an uncle. A few of his brothers had found true happiness with wives and kids. Don't misunderstand, Nate was all about the people he cared about being happy. And marriage was great for some people. He had no plans to rush into a commitment of that magnitude.

When he and his former girlfriend, Mia Chase, had hit the six-month mark of dating, her software job moved to Boulder. She'd told him how much she cared about him and that she didn't want the relationship to end. And that's when the ultimatum came to take their relationship to the next level or end it.

Nate had been honest. He hadn't been ready right then, but that didn't mean he would never be. He didn't share the part about something holding him back. It didn't matter. Mia had balked and it had become clear to him that she'd been expecting a different answer.

A couple of weeks after she'd left, he'd learned the move had been optional. She'd tried to back him against the wall to get him to the altar. Her plan had backfired. To this day, he couldn't understand why she'd done it, but he knew for certain that he'd dodged a bullet. There wasn't much Nate despised more than a liar.

Besides, six months was a long time to spend with the same person. He'd been bored for the last two, but hadn't been able to bring himself to break up with her after she'd told him she was still dealing with the loss of her sister to lymphoma. That, he later found out, had also been a lie.

He hammered the last of the nails and backed out of the crawl space. "That should take care of it."

Chelsea had ushered her daughter into the kitchen and now stood next to him. She'd changed into form-fitting jeans, a blouse and ankle boots. Her hair was slicked back in a ponytail, her brown eyes intent on him. "How'd you do that with Skylar?"

The little nugget, he knew, was in the kitchen, eating with her grandmother and happily chatting about how much fun her day at school was going to be.

"It's magic." Nate's work was done. It was time to take off. He put his hat back on and pulled down on the rim in front.

Chelsea was beautiful. And, under different circumstances, she was exactly the person he'd enjoy getting to know better. But family was sacred to him and he doubted a woman like Chelsea would be happy with what he could offer—a great time in the sack with mutual consent. Besides, the burn marks from his last relationship were fresh and he had no intention of jogging down that same snake-filled path any time soon.

"We're obviously new in town. Last night was our first night in a new house and this morning is not off to a good start," Chelsea said on what seemed like a frustrated sigh.

He already knew, thanks to Linda, she was single. He didn't want to like that fact as much as he did.

"Jacobstown is a great place to bring up a family. Small-town atmosphere. Nice folks," he told her. He also felt the need to warn her about the heifers. "Until a recent crime spree involving heifers, I don't think we knew what crime was."

Her eyes grew wide. "And now?"

"We've had a threat to our livestock. A few animals have been butchered by a man who has been cutting off the hooves of animals. In fact, he just picked up a name, Jacobstown Hacker. You might hear folks mention him." Nate didn't want to go into more details than that but people were on edge and she deserved to know the truth about what was going on.

Her face twisted in a mix of rebuke and sadness. "This sounds like one messed-up individual. Who on earth would get pleasure out of hurting innocent animals?"

"A twisted jerk." Nate couldn't agree more. "Do you have a pet?"

"I promised Skylar a puppy once we get settled," she said on a sigh.

"Might want to think about keeping it inside. There are coyotes to deal with in the country. Not to mention the Texas heat."

"Wouldn't have it any other way." Chelsea's eyes sparked but she didn't mention where she'd moved from.

"Folks from the city are known to drive out to these parts to drop off unwanted dogs. Not sure if you had your heart set on a specific breed, but you can save money if you're willing to care for anything that turns up." Nate thought it was a shame people did that to animals. A domesticated dog, especially a puppy, didn't have the survival skills necessary to outsmart a bobcat or a hungry pack of wolves. Get much farther out and wild boar roamed.

"That's awful." Chelsea frowned and he had no business looking at her pink lips or the freckle on the left side of her mouth.

"If you end up with more than you can handle, give my ranch a call. We have heated and air-conditioned barns for the horses with plenty of room to take care of strays." Nate gave her his personal cell number, just in case.

"I'll keep that in mind."

Part of Nate wanted to volunteer that she call if *she* needed anything. But he knew better. Go down that rabbit hole and what?

He had no idea. Chelsea seemed the opposite of Mia, but first impressions could be deceiving. He'd learned that the hard way, too.

Still fresh from his breakup and betrayal, Nate knew better than to jump back into the dating saddle—no matter how much his heart seemed to have other ideas when it came to the town's newest resident. Casual and consensual sex was another story altogether. He'd had plenty of that in the past few months since the breakup.

Lately, his opinion of it was changing.

"HE WAS NICE." Chelsea's mother winked at her.

"Don't get any ideas," Chelsea warned. She took her daughter's hand, ignoring the disappointment rumbling around in her chest that the cowboy had left. She didn't have time to mess around with an attraction. There was work to do and, for the first time in four years, she felt a twinge of excitement and a whole heap of nervous energy. But it was good.

"You look…" Linda paused. "Happy."

"Aunt Maddie did us a huge favor with this house and the business. There's enough money to get things off the ground. I know it'll be work, but I'm up for it." If she budgeted super tight, they should be okay. Her money was planned down to the penny. There wasn't a whole lot of play, which worried her about her mother's episode this morning. Chelsea hoped the health incident had been brought on by Linda missing her morning medication and not something more serious, such as her condition getting worse.

And just because she'd become expert at handling curve balls didn't mean she wouldn't mind an occasional straight path. What she needed was a fast track to success. But she knew building a business took time.

Shoot. That reminded her. She should've mentioned her business to the cowboy. He seemed like he knew everyone and it wouldn't hurt to start getting word out about her new pizza place that would open in six weeks.

Speaking of which, the delivery men would soon be at her restaurant site to install her fire pit and she needed to get a move on.

Chelsea checked her cell, making sure no one had called. And a little part of her wished Nate Kent would have. There was another text from Renaldo, this time asking if he could come see her new house.

Seriously?

"Ready, Sky?"

Her daughter's eyes brightened as she nodded. "Can we get him?"

"Oh, no, honey. The fireman has to work and be ready to help other people on a moment's notice." Skylar's confused face stared up at Chelsea and her mother laughed. And then it dawned on Chelsea why. "You mean a puppy don't you?" Sky had been asking for a male puppy after reading a popular book about a yellow lab together.

"Uh-huh." Skylar nodded. "What else?"

Linda clucked her tongue and Chelsea refused to react. She wasn't giving in and letting her mother know how embarrassed she was. The woman would have a field day. She might be ill but her mind was sharp—a little too quick-witted for Chelsea's liking.

"Let's get you bundled up," Chelsea said to Skylar. "It's cold outside and the truck heater is taking another day off."

"Maybe *you* should take the day off, Momma." Sky's eyes were huge and they twinkled.

"I have important work to do." It felt good to say that. Even better to mean it.

Renaldo did not get to win. Not as long as Chelsea could help it. If he made good on his promise, she'd never work in another five-star restaurant for the rest of her career.

With the inheritance, she didn't intend to need to.

There was plenty to do and even more to worry about. But a light feeling filled her for the first time in longer than she could remember. Four years ago, she'd held her baby in her arms and wondered how on earth she'd be able to support her. Four years ago, she'd made a promise to that sleeping angel to figure out a way to come out on top. Four years ago, Chelsea had no idea the journey that was about to begin. She'd made it this far and, rather than focus on what she didn't have, she'd decided to be grateful for what she did.

Chelsea retrieved Skylar's winter coat from the same closet that had been a source of trouble this morning. Hair prickled at the base of her neck. She tried to shake off the creepy-crawly feeling but failed. Maybe she'd have concrete poured into that crawl space to seal it off.

"Ready, Sky?" Chelsea turned to find her daughter skipping toward her down the hall, a wide smile on her face. To be a kid again and able to bounce back from every setback in life so fast. Chelsea could learn a thing or two about not holding on to the past, she thought as she wrapped the coat around her daughter.

"Can we go to the man's house?" Skylar's face lit up.

Chelsea didn't have it in her to dash the hope of her child, but she didn't want to set false expectations, either.

"Right now, we need to get you to school. We'll figure out the rest later." Those last six words had become her new mantra.

School drop-off went smoothly and Chelsea figured she owed Nate Kent a pizza on the house at her grand opening considering he was probably the reason. Skylar had met her teacher with an eager smile and most likely the strong hope that Henry would be showing up.

The delivery truck showed within minutes of Chelsea's arrival at what would be her new restaurant. The place needed a major overhaul, and would get it in the coming weeks. The location on Main Street would be perfect and she didn't mind some sweat equity if it meant she could have her own space again.

There was enough room for a dozen four-top tables for guests wanting to dine in. A small construction crew would show up tomorrow to knock out one of the walls to the outside to create a half wall on one side so customers could dine outside with a full view to the inside.

Three hours later, the oven was installed and Chelsea had cleaned out a corner in the back of the restaurant that would make a perfect office. She could have the same contractors put up Sheetrock, leaving space for a window so she could keep an eye on the kitchen.

She had another forty-five minutes before she had to leave to pick up Skylar.

Glancing around, she couldn't help but smile. She was dirty from head to toe from cleaning up the construction zone. But this was progress.

Chelsea picked up the broom. She had time to give the floor another sweep.

How crazy was it that a day could start out like this one had and turn into one of the most gratifying?

She finished sweeping, leaned the broom against the wall and then checked her phone. Another text from Renaldo had come in. If he thought she was going to answer any of these, he was eating fruit off the crazy tree. For a half second she thought about changing her number. It would be a hassle but it might be worth it.

If he kept on, she would have no choice. For now,

she decided not to add any fuel to the fire and see what happened.

Lighter in step, she grabbed her purse and fished out her keys.

It was still light outside at three twenty-five in the afternoon, but not for long. Another couple of hours and it'd be dark. Part of Chelsea hoped that Skylar would be so worn out by her first day that she'd be ready for an early dinner, a hot bath and bed.

Chelsea laughed.

Yeah, right.

That was about as likely as Skylar getting a job and pitching in to pay the bills.

Locking the door to her place—her new restaurant—caused tears to well in her eyes. Happy tears.

She turned toward her pickup. She gasped and took a step back, only to be stopped by the industrial metal door.

Travis's flat smile was more like a sneer.

"Baby, you've been hard to track down."

Chapter Four

"I have no idea where you've been and what you've been doing, but I have a document that says I have no legal ties to you anymore," Chelsea said. Four years of anger, abandonment and betrayal welled inside her, threatening to bubble over. She fisted her hands and readied to draw her knee up, fast and hard, straight to Travis's groin if he took one step closer.

He seemed shorter than before but it was probably her perspective that had changed. At five feet, ten inches, with a decent build, he still paled in comparison with Nate Kent. Travis had sandy-blond hair and hazel eyes. Some people would consider him attractive with the defined jawline and runner's build. Not Chelsea. That ship had sailed the minute she'd seen behind the façade to the real man.

"A man has a right to see his wife and child—"

"*Ex*-wife," she corrected. "And you lost your rights when you disappeared with all of our money and left me with nothing to take care of a newborn."

"People make mistakes," he countered with one

of those smiles that had made her heart flutter years ago. Standing there now, it was hard to know what she'd seen in him. She'd been young and naïve. He'd been a heck of a lot more charming when she hadn't known what a heartless jerk he'd turn out to be.

"Listen, baby—"

"Don't call me that. My name is Chelsea." She'd be damned if she let him get away with any of that sweet talk now. Besides, she'd never been big on being called *baby*. Kids could be manipulated. She was a grown woman, an ex-wife, and had the scars to prove it. No one—and that especially meant Travis—would ever be given the chance take advantage of her again. She was reminded of the old saying "Fool me once, shame on you. Fool me twice, shame on me."

If she fell for that easy charm and smile again, she deserved every moment of heartache that came along with it.

Travis stared at her for an uncomfortable moment before he made a show of glancing around. There was nothing genuine about the look in his eyes. She could see that so clearly now.

"Where's the little one?" he asked.

He didn't know if she'd given birth to a girl or boy. How on earth could a man not know something that important about his own child? "You would know if you'd showed up at the hospital four years ago. Move out of my way. I have plans."

His smile turned into a sneer as she tried to push past him. A dark cloud passed behind his hazel eyes.

"You're mad. I get that. But we had something special, bab—"

She shot him a look so harsh he stopped mid-word.

"Chelsea," he continued. "I did something I shouldn't have, but it can't be too late to be a family. Our child needs a father."

"We'll see about that," was all Chelsea said. She hadn't asked for child support in the divorce and she wondered if he'd even received the paperwork. Of course, he'd had to have by now. A wave of panic washed over her. She imagined the possibility of court battles for custody and the need for a lawyer. She'd never been anxious before Travis. Now she lived with her nerves on the edge. Being broke and bringing up a child on her own did that to her.

And it was great that he was now saying that Skylar was his in the first place. When she'd first told him the news about the pregnancy, he'd accused her of sleeping with one of her employees.

"There's not a judge in Texas who would deny me the right to see my child. You better get used to the idea of seeing me around, because I plan to be in both of your lives." He brought his hand up to touch her face, but she smacked it away before he made contact.

"Don't touch me, Travis," she stated as calmly as she could with her heart hammering against her ribs. She needed to talk to a lawyer to find out her legal rights. "What gives you the right to waltz back into our lives? Where have you been?"

"Alaska," he said. "I went to work on a pipeline so I could save money to pay you back and see if you'd give me another chance."

Okay, her ex was seriously delusional if he thought she would look at him twice let alone consider a reconciliation. He'd have to be delusional or drunk, and she didn't smell alcohol on his breath. If he had been in Alaska and that whole story turned out to be true, she might have to figure out a supervised visitation schedule. How many nights had she held her infant daughter and wished the little girl could grow up with a father?

Too many to count, a voice in the back of her mind said.

But before Travis got a chance with their daughter, Chelsea needed to know he wouldn't disappear again. Her angel deserved a man who stuck around, not someone who popped in and out of her life every four or five years when it was convenient for him.

The timing of his showing up again with Chelsea about to open a restaurant following receiving an inheritance was suspect. None of this exchange was sitting right with her. She figured she could do an easy enough internet search to check out his story. She could make some calls. She'd never filed criminal charges against him for draining their bank account and, technically, the money was as much his as it had been hers. She'd been crazy enough to trust him to put both names on the accounts. He'd showed an interest in her growing company and she'd had a vision of running a family business someday.

"You can start by paying your child the money you stole from us, Travis. Don't waste your time trying to win me back. If you stick around this time and prove you really want to be a father to your child, we can talk about you two meeting. Until then—"

Travis's sneer intensified as he took a threatening step toward her. He was so close she could smell his aftershave, which had been put on with gusto.

Instinctively, Chelsea turned her face to the side and winced. And then she caught herself acting afraid. She remembered that the best way to stop a bully was to confront one.

She turned her face toward his. He grabbed her chin and forced a kiss on her lips before she could push him back a step.

He came at her again, but this time she threw her right knee into his groin.

Travis brought his hands up to the door to brace himself and keep from dropping to the ground. He blew out a couple of sharp breaths as Chelsea tried to duck underneath his arm.

She managed to break away until he spun around and grabbed her by the arm.

"You're hurting me," she said through clenched teeth. She dropped down to her knees, breaking his grip.

"When did you get so mean?" Travis asked through labored breaths as she stood up and side-stepped him.

"Go away, Travis."

"Not until I see my child." He seemed to know

right where to hit her. Four years ago, it was her financial security. Now, money paled in comparison to the need to protect her daughter from harm. She wanted to tell him that would happen as soon as hell froze over.

Checking into her legal rights just became top priority.

She stalked to her truck that was parked on the street, half expecting him to charge up behind her again. This exchange was making her late to pick up Skylar.

Chelsea made it to her pickup and jumped inside. She immediately closed and locked the door. And then she drove around the block a couple of times to make sure Travis was gone and hadn't followed her.

When she was certain he was long gone, she pulled over and let the school know she was running late.

Ten minutes later Chelsea pulled into the parking lot and found a space. It wasn't hard because it was empty. Surprising tears sprang to her eyes. Travis in Skylar's life should be a good thing. He was her father. Knowing what he'd done and what he was capable of doing slammed into Chelsea.

A car pulled into the lot and she watched it all the way until it parked. Relief flooded her when a female stepped out of the driver's side. Chelsea wished she'd taken note of what Travis had driven.

She hurried inside the building. There were two kids besides Skylar, and Chelsea was grateful that she wasn't the last one there.

"I'm so sorry to be late," Chelsea said to the head mistress, Mrs. Bartels.

"She had a great day," Mrs. Bartels informed her. "She was a little shy at first, but that all changed once she got comfortable with the other students."

Normally that kind of news would make Chelsea smile and ease the tension she'd been feeling.

"That's really good to hear," Chelsea finally said. "Thank you."

"Would you like me to walk you to her classroom?" Mrs. Bartels asked.

The female from the parking lot rushed in.

"Hello, Mrs. Stanley," Mrs. Bartels said.

"Hi, Elaine," the woman responded. "How'd he do today?"

Chelsea excused herself. She needed to see her baby, to know that Skylar was okay, even though she already did on some level. If there'd been trouble, Mrs. Bartels would've phoned. And, besides, Travis didn't know he had a daughter let alone where she was.

Skylar's eyes lit up when she saw her mother step into the room. Her little face broke into a wide smile. "Mommy!"

Chelsea made eye contact with the teacher, Mrs. Eaton, who smiled her approval.

Dropping to her knees, she welcomed the little angel who had flown over to her. Those tiny arms wrapped around Chelsea's neck brought an unexpected tear.

"I'm so happy to see you." She held her little girl a bit tighter.

"I had fun. I colored a picture of an elephant and rode a real bike." Skylar's enthusiasm for her day eased some of Chelsea's guilt for being away from her so long.

"It sounds like you were very busy," Chelsea agreed. She pulled back a little to look into her daughter's eyes. "And you get to come back tomorrow."

Skylar's face nearly burst from smiling so hard as she nodded. "Do you think he'll be here?"

A wave of panic ripped through Chelsea. There was no way Skylar could be talking about Travis. "Who?"

Her gaze darted toward Mrs. Eaton for an answer.

"You know," Skylar said, making eyes at her mother. "The fireman."

"Probably not, sweetie." Relief washed over Chelsea. "But all your new friends will be. Now go get your coat."

Before Skylar trotted away, she said, "He was right about Henry. My teacher has a frog."

Mrs. Stanley came into the room and the little boy who'd been sitting at the same coloring table as Skylar perked up.

"Hey, buddy," Mrs. Stanley said, bending to one knee. "Are you ready?"

He dutifully walked to his cubby and got his things. Skylar struggled with hers.

Chelsea walked over to help her daughter with

her coat as a man's voice from the hallway shot through her. She sucked in a burst of air and spun around.

Mrs. Eaton looked at Chelsea, confusion stamped on her forehead. A man in a janitor's shirt nodded and walked in to empty the trash.

"Sorry," Chelsea mumbled as she led Skylar out of the classroom, down the hallway and into the parking lot. It was dark outside now and she watched wearily as every car drove by while she buckled her daughter into the car seat.

CHELSEA PULLED INTO her driveway and her heart clenched. An unfamiliar truck was parked on the pad next to the house. Complete panic was a stalking panther coming up from behind. Chelsea used the rearview mirror to glance at her daughter, who was strapped into her car seat in the back.

What if Travis knew where they lived?

Chelsea cursed the wave of fear threatening to suck her under. She'd already dealt with him once today and wasn't sure she could take another round. She couldn't tell Skylar to stay in the truck alone and nothing in her wanted to go inside to see who was there.

She grabbed the gearshift, ready to put the truck in Reverse on a moment's notice. Maybe she could wait it out. She could park down the street and see who the truck belonged to.

"Momma, are we going inside?" Skylar looked at

Chelsea with the most adorable albeit incredulous look on her four-year-old face.

"Maybe in just a minute, sweetheart. I'm not sure who that truck belongs to," Chelsea admitted.

"What if Nanna is sick again and needs our help?" Skylar asked.

In Chelsea's panic about her run-in with Travis, the episode with her mother this morning had slipped her mind. Well, that got Chelsea moving and her mind spinning.

"You're right. Let's go inside. But hold Mommy's hand and stay behind me until I say it's okay." Skylar was old enough to unbuckle her car seat strap. Chelsea held the door open so the little girl could climb out.

Every step toward the front door caused Chelsea's heart to pound faster against her rib cage. Tamping down her fears, she squeezed Skylar's hand once they got onto the porch.

Skylar took her mother's advice, hiding behind her leg.

Chelsea couldn't bring herself to put her key in the lock.

"Can I do it, Momma?" Skylar always wanted to be the one to do the honors.

Normally, Chelsea wouldn't have a problem letting her. The place had one of those old-fashioned skeleton keys and she was pretty sure the door, lock and key were original to the house. The place needed some updating once Chelsea got on her feet. For now, it was her own personal piece of paradise. The thought of Travis invading her territory made her downright furious. He'd taken so much already. He didn't get to take this.

Chelsea worked up enough courage to open that door and face whatever was inside.

The sound of a man's laugh from inside the house washed over her. The familiar timbre sent warmth spilling down her back. Nate Kent.

His laughter was quickly followed by her mother's.

Chelsea walked into the hallway. A chill hit her. The heater had better not be out. The weather was turning and January in Texas could bring all kinds of cold snaps.

Her nerves were beyond fried at this point, even though her rebellious stomach freefell at the sight of Nate standing in her kitchen. Her mother was no-where in sight but Chelsea could hear the woman's voice and Nate was angled toward the kitchen table. Thoughts of her mother's episode this morning struck hard.

"Is everything okay in here?" Chelsea asked the handsome near stranger. It had been an awful day and she didn't need to make it worse by worrying about her mother. But what if something had happened to her mother?

Nate turned to look at Chelsea, causing a hundred butterflies to release in her stomach.

Under normal circumstances, she'd like to spend time getting to know Nate Kent. But the "normal" ship had sailed years ago for Chelsea. And no matter how wonderful someone seemed at first or how good-looking—and this guy hit it out of the park with his looks—she'd never truly trust another man again. Travis had done a number on her. Part of her realized that by allowing that experience to color the rest of her life, she was letting him win.

"Hey, mister." Skylar darted around Chelsea's leg and ran toward Nate. She'd never seen her little girl be so welcoming to a stranger before and a part of her wondered if the fast friendship had anything to do with the fact that Nate was a man. Was Skylar missing having a male figure in her life?

Chelsea was grateful for her mother's help and presence in her daughter's life. Even while sick and requiring attention herself, the woman had been nothing short of a lifesaver. Linda McGregor had kept Chelsea from the staggering loneliness in those early days of Travis's disappearing. She'd loved Skylar with all her heart from the moment the child had been born. And she'd pitched in to care for the little angel, which had allowed Chelsea to get back on her feet.

Working nights had made it all possible. Chelsea left for work at four. Skylar ate dinner an hour later and was in bed by seven. She'd always been an early riser and Chelsea was pretty certain she didn't sleep for Skylar's first three years of life. Those early years weren't easy, but the Three Musketeers—as her mother had called them—had made it work.

Looking back, she kicked herself for not seeing through Travis sooner. He'd been charming and seemed genuine with his admission of falling for her even though he'd said he didn't think it was possible with his background. He'd told her about a loveless childhood where he'd been bounced around from family member to family member when his mother's "nerves" were shot. He'd said it was code for when she had to go into rehab again.

Chelsea had never met his mother, so she had no reason to doubt his claims. He'd explained that his mother and his family couldn't come to their wedding because his mother had gone off on a bender. Chelsea had fallen for his lies.

After he'd left her and she'd searched for him, she found out that his mother was married to a pastor in a small town outside Little Rock. Chelsea'd been working long hours as her business expanded or maybe she would've been sharper. Lack of sleep didn't always yield the best judgment.

Nate dropped down to his knees so he was almost eye level with Skylar, causing Chelsea's heart to give another inappropriate flip. It was probably his training as a volunteer firefighter that had him so good with kids and not because he had some instant connection to Sky. Did part of her want Skylar to be able to connect with the handsome stranger?

She could admit that was true. Chelsea hoped her daughter would be able to trust men at some point. She'd always shied away from them and, deep down, Chelsea feared it would always be that way. There was something so totally different about Nate Kent, though. He was special.

With kids, that little voice quickly added.

"What are you doing here?" Skylar asked, fist planted on her hip like she was owed an explanation. Kids were so straightforward.

Chelsea sighed, wishing the same was true for adults.

"Your grandmother called and asked to see me," he answered.

Chelsea's cheeks burned from embarrassment because she suspected her mother was up to no good. "Mom. Is everything okay?"

"Better now." Her mother's cheeky smile told Chelsea everything she needed to know about what was happening.

Chelsea shot Linda a warning look when Nate's gaze dropped to Skylar.

"I was only saying this gentleman was a big help." Her mother gave a not-so-innocent shrug. "Someone threw a rock through the living room window and I was too scared to sit here alone until you got home."

"You should've called me, Mother." Chelsea held back from scolding the woman.

"I didn't want to bother you and this nice man did say this morning that I should call if I needed anything," her mother said.

"I meant it, too. It's not always easy being the new kid in town," Nate noted.

Especially one with an ex who seemed intent on bringing her down.

As she thought about the broken window, a question begged an answer.

Had Travis figured out where she lived?

Chapter Five

Chelsea tried to mask her panic as she shivered against the cold. "Someone threw a rock through the window?" She hadn't noticed any broken glass.

"Yes. At least, I believe it was a rock," her mother supplied. "It just happened."

Chelsea had already started toward the living room.

"I didn't want to upset you and I thought we could have this all fixed up before you got home so you wouldn't worry," her mother said. "It's no big deal."

Those words banged around in Chelsea's head. Sure, it was nothing to worry about if a couple of kids were playing a prank by tossing a rock at a window and running away. Her mother had no idea that Travis had resurfaced. Chelsea couldn't bring herself to mention him in front of Skylar. Instead of dwelling on the fact that a four-year-old had never met her father, Chelsea marched into the living room and scanned the floor for an object hard enough to break glass.

The window that had been broken was on the east

side of the house, facing the parking pad. It was the bottom right panel. Chelsea didn't see that when she'd driven up. Dark grey clouds covered the sun even though it wouldn't officially be dark outside for another couple of hours.

The trail from the broken window to the location of the rock was an easy trajectory. Chelsea dropped down to her knees with a little more force than she expected. She started to pick up the rock, struggling against the onslaught of emotion threatening to unravel her tight grip.

"Hold on." Nate's calm, compassionate voice washed over her and through her and all she could think about was that it had been too long since she'd been on a date. Her stomach quivered at his voice and she could only imagine what would happen if he touched her.

Chelsea quashed the inappropriate thought.

"Whoever did this should be prosecuted. I'll call the sheriff." Nate palmed his cell phone as Chelsea stood.

"I'm hungry, Momma," Skylar said.

"I'll take her into the kitchen and fix her something to eat," Linda said, taking Skylar by the hand.

"Thank you. I'll be right in as soon as I figure out how to board this window up before we freeze tonight," Chelsea said.

Nate shot a look of apology and it dawned on her why. She couldn't touch that, either. There might be fingerprints.

"I'll stay right here," Nate said into the phone after providing the details to the sheriff.

Those words kept Chelsea from complete panic. She liked Nate and maybe it was because she needed her faith restored in men. After Travis, and then later her boss, she wasn't thrilled with the opposite sex.

"Thank you for sticking around," she said to Nate. "I promise we're normally pretty boring people."

He looked at her like he was looking through her. "Somehow, I doubt that."

She started to ask what he meant but he cut her off by putting his hand in the air.

"You're a great mother to that little girl. It's easy to see that she's loved and well cared for. If rumors can be trusted, you're about to open a gourmet pizza restaurant in town. You're smart. I take one look at you and can see that you're beautiful. I highly doubt that your life is boring," he said.

Did he just call her beautiful? Chelsea flushed red-hot. She hated that her cheeks always gave her away.

A knock sounded at the door, interrupting her embarrassing moment. Her mother would laugh if she'd heard the silence after Nate's remark.

"I'll be right back," was all she could muster to say as she held up her finger like she was telling him to wait right there.

Chelsea walked out of the room and to the front door. She stood at the closed door and for a split second feared Travis would be standing on the other side. Now that he'd returned, she wondered if she'd always have the feeling he could be on the other side of every unopened door. A chill raced down her back.

She tamped down her unease and opened the door. Thankfully, the sheriff stood on her porch.

"Good evening, ma'am. I'm Zach McWilliams." He stuck out his hand.

Chelsea took the offering and introduced herself. She could feel Nate's presence behind her and that frustrated her. She didn't want to have a visceral reaction to this man or any other.

"Come on in, Sheriff." She stepped aside.

"Thanks for coming, Zach," Nate said. She wondered if everyone in town was on a first-name basis. She liked the thought of neighbors who knew each other. That was a large part of the appeal of moving to a small town. She envisioned people helping each other and not throwing rocks through a window.

Nate and the sheriff resembled each other enough for her to do a double take.

Nate must've caught on to her confusion. "Zach is my cousin."

In her estimation, Nate won the genetic lotto between the two of them. Zach was good-looking, just not in the same manner as Nate. There was something extra special about Nate. She shelved the thought as she led Zach into her living room.

"Rock came through that window over there." She motioned toward the east-facing window.

"You're new here." Zach stated the obvious.

"That's right," she confirmed.

"That's no way to be welcomed to Jacobstown," Zach said. "We're normally a friendlier town than this."

Zach and Nate exchanged glances.

What was that about?

"WE'VE HAD SOME trouble at a couple of ranches." Nate picked up on Chelsea's hesitation.

"Oh, yeah? Like what?" She stopped in the middle of the room and folded her arms. A look of fear passed through her eyes.

Nate picked up on the look and decided to ask more about what caused it later.

"Animals have had hooves butchered," Zach told her.

"Nate mentioned that. Who would do that? Teens?" she asked.

"This is gruesome and cruel. It's happened enough times and at enough places to put people in town on edge and make them worried there's more to come," Zach said. "It's way over the head of teens."

"Is that why you wanted to call the sheriff over my broken window?" She looked from Zach to Nate.

"Something like this is unusual here. Most folks are friendly and welcome strangers. No one used to lock their doors. Heck, half the town would leave keys in their car while they were parked to run into a store or into the county building. Not anymore. We have a panic mentality going on with a few and others are nervous. They aren't as accepting of new people. We're keeping an eye on anything out of the ordinary that happens. This qualifies," Zach informed.

There was something about this rock business that rubbed Nate the wrong way. Sure, people were on edge and, sometimes, they did something stupid. But folks in Jacobstown didn't pick on strangers. The town had a reputation for going out of its way to make others feel welcome.

Chelsea moving to town had nothing to do with the heifers.

"Are you from Texas?" Zach began the routine-sounding questions that Nate had heard from his cousin during investigations.

"Yes. Houston," she added.

Nate bowed his head and pulled out his cell, pretending he wasn't too interested in her answers.

"What about a spouse?" Zach continued.

"I was married once." Chelsea lowered her voice when she spoke. Nate glanced up and saw that she was staring at the floor. "I'm not anymore."

"Have you been in a fight with anyone or does anyone have a reason to want to harm you?" Zach asked.

A pair of footsteps came from the hallway. The heavy pair, Nate noticed, belonged to Skylar. Nate always marveled at how heavy someone three or four feet tall could walk in comparison to an adult.

Linda had her granddaughter's hand.

"I'll take her upstairs and give her a bath," the older woman said.

"Thank you, Mom." Chelsea looked to Zach as she shivered. "Any chance I can board up that window soon?"

"Yes, ma'am." Zach pulled out his phone and sent a text. "I just let my deputy know to drop what he's doing and come dust so you can cover the window."

Under different circumstances, Nate wouldn't mind offering to keep her warm. The thought was totally inappropriate given the current situation. Besides, he couldn't see himself trusting another woman for a while. He needed a cooling-off period after Mia.

Normally, Nate could spot a liar from a mile away. Mia had put on a convincing show. He was still disappointed in himself for allowing the relationship to go on as long as it had. He'd developed a soft spot lately that he didn't care much for. Mia had toyed with his emotions and used that weakness against him. Between that and the mutilated heifers, Nate had been in a lousy mood.

Little Skylar had changed that this morning. Being around Chelsea and her family was different than what he was used to. But then, Nate didn't normally do overnight stays or meet-the-families. Even more reason to be frustrated with his lapse in judgment when it came to Mia.

Zach's questions were a low murmur in the background. Nate's ears perked up when his cousin asked where Chelsea's ex-husband lived.

Chelsea's gaze shot up from staring at the floor to the staircase.

"I have no idea," she said, her voice low, like she didn't want her daughter to hear. "He disappeared while I was pregnant and I haven't seen or heard from him in four years. And then a few hours ago, he showed up at my restaurant out of the blue. No warning. He just appeared and started making demands."

Zach perked up with this information, too. Nate had a feeling their piqued interest in her response was for very different reasons.

"Did he say what he was doing there after all this time?" Zach's brow knitted together.

"Yes. He said that he wanted me back and wanted to see his child." Her tone sounded incredulous.

Nate couldn't help but look at her. What did he expect to see? For some strange reason, part of him wanted to know if she was still in love with her ex. Based on the tense lines across her forehead, the answer was *no*.

That shouldn't give him pleasure. This was a family, and that should always take precedence over everything else. If there was a way to heal one, Nate would be the last person to stand in the way. There were a few exceptions to that rule. A man who physically or emotionally abused a woman or child didn't deserve to have either.

"Did he say why he left in the first place?" Zach asked after taking down the name she supplied.

Chelsea looked like answering would put her in physical pain.

Zach apologized for the line of questioning before

continuing. "I need to assess any threat to you, your daughter, and anyone else in town this person could see as a barrier to getting what he wants."

"He didn't give an excuse as to why he disappeared that day. I was in the hospital giving birth to our daughter while he cleaned out our bank accounts and bankrupted my successful small business. He did say that he wanted a reunion. I made my position clear on that." Her fisted hand on her hip coupled with the stress creases around her eyes made her stance clear to anyone who paid attention to body language.

"My apologies, ma'am. Can you tell me what happened next?" Zach asked.

"I got in my truck, made sure he didn't follow me and then drove to my daughter's school to pick her up. I was late on her first day." She looked to the right and high. She was being honest. Knowing if someone, anyone, was lying to him had taken on a new importance since Mia. He'd been watching for signs of truthfulness every time he listened to someone speak. Honesty meant even more to him.

"Approximately how long did it take to pick up your daughter?" Zach asked.

"Enough time for him to come here and throw a rock through the window," she stated. "He was my first thought."

"Is there anyone else?" Zach asked.

"My former boss threatened me if I quit. He's also sent a few texts since I moved, asking to come visit." She pulled her cell phone out and placed it on her flat hand. "I haven't answered because I'd like to move on from that part of my life."

She was beautiful. It was easy to see why someone would ask her out, but what Nate was hearing sounded like downright harassment. He clenched his back teeth. Give him five minutes alone with those jerks and they'd come out with a new respect for all women.

Zach took down the name and information of the kitchen boss she'd worked for. "What made you decide to move to Jacobstown?"

"This house was a gift," she said. "My great-aunt, Maddie Barstock, owned this house and the downtown property where I'm opening my restaurant. She left them both to me in her will. It seemed like a great way to start over, so we packed up and moved. She also gave me her business downtown."

"You and your great-aunt were close?" Zach asked.

"Strangely enough, we weren't. I mean, I didn't really know her. She and my mother weren't close and my mother's been sick the past few years. I didn't even realize I had a great-aunt on my mom's side."

"She must've remembered you," Zach stated. He looked up at Nate and it was clear the two were thinking the same thing.

"Didn't Ms. Barstock move to assisted living in Austin to be closer to family?" Nate asked.

"It's been a few years, but I remember hearing something like that." Zach pinched the bridge of his nose. It was a habit he'd picked up in the last couple of years when he tried to reach back in his memory. He seemed to pick up on the earlier conversation thread. "It'll be nice to have a new place to eat. That end of the square has been empty too long and I've had to watch out for teenagers there."

"I plan to put the building to good use," Chelsea said, and there was so much pride in those words.

There was something special about Chelsea and Skylar. Nate found himself wanting to help the single mother. With an ex showing up—an ex who was a criminal—and a former boss who seemed hell-bent on keeping tabs on her, she could use an extra set of eyes to keep her safe. Nate would be there as much as she wanted him to be because he'd also picked up on the fact that she wasn't the most trusting when it came to the opposite sex.

A knock interrupted the conversation.

Chelsea gasped and then apologized for her nerves.

Zach and Nate followed her to the foyer just in case her ex had decided to pay a visit, but Deputy Long stood on the porch when she opened the door. She let him in and he went right to work in the living room, wearing his gloves and using fingerprint powder to lift a print from the window.

"I'll check outside." Zach excused himself. Rain threatened and it was dark outside, making it feel much later than it was. Nate and Chelsea stepped out onto the porch.

Chelsea's little girl ran outside. "Momma, I can see my breath."

"Okay, sweetie. Go inside and I'll be right there," Chelsea said.

"Nanna said I had to go with her to her room to play." The little girl frowned.

"That's probably a good idea. Don't you agree?" Chelsea's smile twisted Nate's insides. She was being strong for her daughter and it sounded like she'd been through a lot. From her statement, she'd grown a business that had been bankrupted right under her nose. She'd then gone to work for someone else, who'd also turned out to be a total jerk.

And that brought Nate to another line of thinking. Her ex was in town. He might be trying to scare her by tossing a rock through the window. Or maybe the chef had taken a ride to Jacobstown and was outside waiting for everyone to leave. He'd ask Zach to check into the whereabouts of the Houston chef tonight. It would be easy enough to call the restaurant where he worked. If the guy had taken the day off, he could've made the drive.

Reality crashed down. This wasn't Nate's case or his business. Once he helped board up her window and arranged for a replacement, his job would be done here.

In fact, it was late, but he was owed a favor by Bill Staller, a local contractor. Boarding up the window would let out too much heat. The house was old, drafty.

What She Did

Nate excused himself. He walked over to his truck to make the call.

Bill answered on the first ring. "What can I do for you?"

"I need a favor." The truth was that Nate had kept Bill working for several winters. Bill had asked a dozen times to repay Nate in some way. Nate couldn't think of a better repayment than using the favor to help someone else. Of course, Nate would pay for the window. He wouldn't stick Bill with that price tag. Since the whole house needed energy-efficient windows, he'd pay to have that done, too. It was the least he could do for the struggling little family.

Chelsea seemed like the kind of person who had too much pride to admit she might need a helping hand.

Would she reject it?

Chapter Six

The sheriff had finished taking her statement. The window had been professionally fixed. The night had turned into the next day.

"I can't thank you enough for your help." Chelsea meant it, too. Nate Kent had already helped her daughter this morning and now this. It was too much.

"All part of the job," he said like it was nothing.

It meant a lot to her.

"I'm embarrassed to admit that I fell for a class-A jerk." Saying it out loud didn't make her feel any better, either. How many nights had Chelsea lain awake in bed tossing and turning, willing to give her right arm if she could just go to sleep and stop churning over her mistake? Dozens?

She looked over at Nate, expecting a reaction, a smirk, a look of disdain, or for him to look down on her. Instead, she found a sympathetic smile.

"I think we've all been there at least once in our lives," he said.

She gave him a look that said she didn't believe he'd ever fall into a trap like that.

"What? I'm no different than the next guy." He put his hand in air in the surrender position.

"Right." The sound that came out of her mouth was half chortle, half snort.

"What does that mean?" he asked.

Chelsea could tell that she'd insulted him. "I'm sorry. In no way was I trying to offend you. It's just that you're gorgeous and smart—" She shot him an apologetic look. "It's hard to see how you could have any problems."

She regretted the words as soon as they left her mouth. It was too late to reel them in. He was already on his feet, a storm gathering behind his eyes.

"Your mind is made up. In my experience, it would do no good to try to convince you otherwise." He walked into the kitchen and set his coffee cup down on the counter.

It had only taken a hot minute for her to make a mess of things.

"Is apologizing enough to stop you from hating me?" She realized just how shallow those words were, especially since he'd been nothing but kind to her. Stress was starting to show through and she didn't like the person on display. She'd like to blame Travis, but that wasn't fair. She was in charge of her actions. No one forced her to do or to say anything.

Chelsea was developing feelings for Nate that she didn't want. She was tired and her mother's health weighed heavily on her mind.

"I'm an idiot," she said to Nate's back as he started toward the door. "You're helping me and you've been nothing but nice to Skylar and my mother. I have no right to make judgments about your life. Especially since I don't really know anything about your life."

He didn't immediately turn around and that was the first clue at how badly she might've insulted him.

Pushing through her own walls proved more difficult than she expected. She walked over to him and placed a hand on his arm. "Nate, I'm the jerk here. Please don't be offended by what I said. It's not you. It's me."

He turned on that note and backed her up a step. "I think I understand what's going on."

"You do? Mind cluing me in?" she asked.

"You're scared." His hand rested on the counter. She blinked at him. "Of what?"

"Not of *what...of who.*" He caught her gaze and held on to it.

"I'm not scared of you, Nate. If that's what you're thinking," she stammered. "You've been nothing but helpful."

His smile was devastating. Good-looking was almost an insult to say about a man as gorgeous as Nate. He had that animal magnetism she'd heard about but rarely seen. His piercing steel eyes and carved-from-granite jawline coupled with thick, curly, dark hair made for one seriously hot package.

The man worked out. His body was defined in places
she didn't even realize there could be muscles.

"If not me, then this." He brought his hand up to
her chin and tilted her mouth toward his.

The truth was that she'd thought about kissing
him far too often for her own good since she'd met
him. It was uncharacteristic for her to have such an
immediate and demanding reaction. If she had any
sense, she'd push him away and let him walk out the
door before things went too far.

But she *wanted* him to touch her, *wanted* to feel
his lips moving against hers, *wanted* his hands to
roam freely on her body. She tried to convince herself the only reason her body craved his touch was
that she hadn't really been touched in too long.

That annoying voice inside her head called her
out. *You want Nate.*

Nate was handsome and charming—but not in a
polished and premeditated manner—and real. That
same annoying voice reminded her there was something unavailable about him, too. Was that part of
the attraction?

At this point, Chelsea didn't know or care. Her
body hummed with desire for the handsome cowboy.
She brought her hands up to his chest. Instead of
pushing him away, which would be the smart move,
she let her fingertips run along the muscled ridges.

His lips pressed against hers, causing a jolt of
electricity to envelop her, pinging through her body
and seeking an outlet. When there was none, the vi-

bration hummed, gaining urgency as she gripped his shoulders.

She parted her lips to allow better access and he teased his tongue inside her mouth. Her lips fused with his in a bone-melting kiss. She'd heard about kisses so intense they weakened the knees, but the reality of one was far different, far more intense and pleasurable than anything she'd experienced.

There was so much passion in that one kiss that she melted against his strong, hard body. With her breasts flush against his chest, he released a primal groan. His hands dropped to her waist and he looped them around until they rested on the small of her back.

Her pulse skyrocketed as his large hands splayed across her back.

And this was a runaway train that needed stopping. Yet there was nothing inside Chelsea that wanted to stop kissing Nate. And that was a big problem. Panic gripped her because thinking about the effect of this kiss on her life was the equivalent of a bucket of cold water being poured on her.

She pulled back, forehead to forehead, giving herself enough space to let her ragged breathing stabilize before she stepped away from him.

The sizzle in that kiss had been missing from every kiss in her entire life.

Chelsea was in trouble. She didn't do curl-her-toes kisses anymore. Although, to be fair, this one had melted her bones more than curled her toes.

And there was nothing premeditated about it.

NATE STOOD IN the kitchen a second longer than he should have, locked in eye contact with Chelsea. Kissing her had been an impulse. One he should regret.

In the moment, he'd gone all caveman and ignored logic and better judgment. He hadn't made a mistake like that since he'd reached voting age. Letting his emotions run away with him wasn't something the adult Nate Kent usually did. That glittery look in Chelsea's eyes had him like a moth to a flame.

He tried to tell himself that he'd done it to erase Mia from his thoughts. Normally, bouncing back from a relationship wasn't a problem. It probably had a lot to do with the fact that Nate didn't *do* relationships in the first place. Had he let his guard down with Mia?

Ever since losing his parents and his family changing, Nate had felt off balance.

Time to correct his mistakes.

"Bill has your number. He'll call to make arrangements to replace the rest of the windows," he said to Chelsea.

"I'll get my checkbook," Chelsea said, holding up a finger.

"That's not necessary," Nate said.

"Oh? How's that?" The confused crinkle in her forehead was sexy as hell.

Nate forced his gaze away from it.

"It's covered," was all he said. He didn't want to go into detail as to why he felt the need to personally pay for new windows for the drafty old house. It could use more updates that he was fairly certain Chelsea would insist on covering herself.

"How? I haven't had a chance to set up homeowner's insurance," she stated.

"It's covered. There's nothing to pay." He hoped she'd leave it at that. He didn't know why he'd made the offer, except that when she'd spoken about her ex, he hadn't liked the look of fear in her eyes and he'd wanted to prove that not all men were jerks. "Have you thought about a security system?"

"Here in Jacobstown?" Again, the brows knitted. "I didn't think I'd need one."

"Never hurts to have a little extra security." He didn't want to say that she already had her hands full with a four-year-old and an ill mother. Linda had already told him how hard Chelsea was working to get back on her feet.

Nate wanted to offer a helping hand.

"I'll think about it." She had a lot on her plate financially, he could read it in her eyes. "I meant to mention this morning that the grand opening for the restaurant will be in six weeks if all goes well. You seem to know a lot of people."

Nate grunted and smiled at that one.

"I'd appreciate help spreading word about the opening," she continued.

"Not a problem. Folks in this town will know by morning that there's a new family in town and they'll probably know more about your business than you want them to by week's end." He couldn't help but smile. Living in Jacobstown was like that. Folks looked after each other. "Not a whole lot changes around here. They'll be lining up to experience something new come opening day."

"That's a relief." She blew out a breath.

"I'd best be on my way. Ranch work starts early in the mornings—" he checked the watch on his wrist.

Chelsea gasped. "You have two jobs?"

"Technically, just one, and it's more way of life than occupation," he said. He was glad her earlier tension had subsided some, unless he counted the chemistry pinging between them. That had been on overdrive ever since the kiss.

"What do you do on the ranch?" she asked, leaning her slender hip against the kitchen counter.

Lucky counter. It was easy to talk to Chelsea even though Nate wasn't normally a man of many words.

"Everything," he attested, which was true. He tagged and recorded calf births, rode fences and cleaned stalls, just like everyone else.

"Surely there's a primary responsibility. What's your job title?" she asked.

"Owner."

Chelsea seemed taken back by the admission. For the life of Nate, he couldn't figure out why.

"Is there something wrong with me owning a ranch?" He tried to hide the defensiveness in his voice.

"No. Not really," she said too fast. She'd picked

up on his emotion. "It's just you work as a fire-fighter—"

"Volunteer," he corrected. He understood now. "I don't take a salary for that."

"Oh." The look on her face made her seem even more confused now. Like she couldn't imagine who would run a ranch *and* volunteer.

"This is a small town and we all have to do our part to keep it running. In fairness, I own the ranch with five siblings and we all work the cattle and the land. I volunteer as a firefighter because it gets me off the ranch and I like the distraction.

"Speaking of which, I'd better grab a few hours of shut-eye before my workday starts," he finally said.

Chelsea's face was unreadable. He couldn't tell if she thought he was crazy or noble. And, for some odd reason, it bothered him more than he wanted to admit.

"I can't thank you enough for everything you've done for us." There was a finality in her tone. Like the two would never see each other again.

"Not a problem," he said before leaving.

Inside his truck, he maneuvered around her pickup and out of the drive. On the street, he used the hands-free feature to call Zach.

"What do you think about the McGregor case?" he asked his cousin after perfunctory greetings.

"Wish I knew. I hope it's not someone from town," Zach admitted. "Could be her ex. I'm check-ing motels as we speak to see if he checked into one nearby."

"Throwing a rock through the window bothers me," Nate said.

"How so?" Zach asked.

"Her ex didn't seem to have a problem confronting her head-on earlier. Why chicken out now and break a window in order to scare her?" Nate didn't believe the rock thrower was the same person.

"That crossed my mind, too," Zach conceded. "I'm heading over to the Last Bite Diner near the expressway. You want to come talk this through?"

"Yeah, sure. You headed there now?" Nate asked.

"On my way. I need a place to sit down and make a few calls. There won't be anyone else there at this hour," Zach stated.

Nate ended the call and headed west toward the diner. He was too wired to sleep anyway and that kiss kept overtaking his thoughts. He didn't want to remember how sweet Chelsea's rosy lips felt pressed against his. Or how much better coffee tasted on them. He forced his thoughts onto the road and away from the glittery look in her eyes that had sent him down that path in the first place.

The urge to kiss Chelsea had been a physical ache. Nate didn't want to get too inside his head about the pull toward her. She was an intelligent and attractive woman. She had a good head on her shoulders and had created a successful business. Under normal circumstances, she was the kind of woman he'd want to get to know better. Nate almost laughed. Okay, that wasn't entirely true. Under normal circumstances, he'd want a lot of amazing sex with no strings attached. An option that was clearly not possible with Chelsea, considering she had a child and he got the impression the woman didn't do one-night stands.

Another reason that kiss couldn't happen again. Nate didn't have more than one night to offer.

Kissing her had been bad judgment on his part. He wouldn't go down that road again.

Chapter Seven

Ten minutes later, Nate pulled into a parking spot at the diner. He'd been unsuccessful at not thinking about Chelsea's situation. Her ex showing up out of the blue troubled Nate. She said the two had been apart four years, starting from literally the day Skylar was born.

It made Nate all kinds of angry that a man would walk out on his own child. To never lay eyes on that child was another gut punch. If Nate had had a kid, he would be there just like his parents had been for him and his siblings.

Zach pulled into the parking spot next to Nate, jarring him from his thoughts. He turned off the ignition and stepped out of his truck. He rounded it and noted there was a car parked at the side of the building. Nate couldn't help but notice that Zach had seen it, too.

They both seemed to catch on to the fact that the plates were from Louisiana.

They greeted each other before walking into the restaurant.

A lone diner had positioned himself at the breakfast counter. He huddled over his plate, not bothering to look at the men. There was something familiar about him. He was of medium build and height, with light hair from the back. He had the carriage of someone who worked in an office all day rather than outside.

"Who is that?" Zach asked with an arched brow as he took a seat in the corner booth.

Liesel came over with a fresh carafe of coffee and set it on the table. "Howdy, boys. I know why you're awake—" she motioned toward Zach "—but what's got you up in the middle of the night, cowboy?"

The place was small and had its name on top of the roof in big red lights. Inside, there was a row of booths that stretched down the middle of the room, a counter on the right that ran the length of the place and a few tables to the left.

Liesel had worked at the diner since there'd been a diner, so maybe fifteen years. She kept tabs on most goings-on in Jacobstown given that people came through at all hours of the night. Jacobstown didn't have bartenders, it had Liesel. She poured their coffees.

"Thank you," Nate said as he picked up his cup. He took a sip and immediately thought about how much better coffee tasted when he tasted it on Chelsea.

"Why does he seem familiar?" Zach asked Liesel.

"Who? Him?" She glanced at the counter seater, like there was another option.

"Yes. I know him from somewhere," Zach added.

"That's the Barstock widow's boy, Reggie," she muttered. "He hasn't been around here in ages. He never did come visit his momma even when she died. Said he ain't staying, either."

"Oh, yeah?" Zach had the look on his face that Nate recognized.

His cousin stood, his gaze locked onto the lone diner. "I apologize in advance for leaving you high and dry, Nate. You might be eating alone tonight."

"No problem here. I can always order to go and bring it to your office," Nate offered.

"BLT's the best here. Would you mind ordering me one with the sweet potato fries?" Zach said to Nate even though Liesel was standing right next to them.

"I'll make it two and be there to eat with you in fifteen minutes," Nate said. "But right now I plan to make sure this guy doesn't try any funny business with you."

There was something guilty-looking about the man at the breakfast counter that rubbed Nate the wrong way.

Zach walked toward the lone diner, stopping behind him. "Mind if I sit?"

"The whole place is empty. Can't you find another place to cop a squat?" Reggie didn't look up, didn't make eye contact.

"I'd like to sit here and talk to you. Or we could head down to my office if you'd be more comfortable there." Zach didn't waver.

"I didn't do nothing wrong," Reggie said.

There was something guilty about him. Nate couldn't put his finger on it, but the guy looked like he'd been caught with his hand in the cookie jar.

A picture was emerging. Didn't Chelsea say that she'd inherited the house and business from her great-aunt? A rock had been thrown in her window on her second night in town and Reggie Barstock, whose mother stood him up for the inheritance, makes an appearance?

Nate wanted to follow this through to its conclusion because he would like to be the one to ease Chelsea's fears. The look he'd seen on her face when she'd talked about her ex didn't sit well with him and his thoughts kept drifting to the little family on Sycamore.

"Who said you did?" Zach asked, leaning against the stool next to Reggie. "I thought we could talk. You're the Barstock boy."

Reggie, Nate knew, had been two grades ahead of him. That might as well have been in another town for how much interaction Nate had had with him. Reggie would've been in the same grade as Nate's older brother, Deacon, though. Nate made a mental note to circle back to ask Deacon about Reggie.

Maddie Barstock had been a saint. Her reputation had been golden. Her one and only son had been trouble, best as Nate could recall. The guy had disappeared after high school, which wasn't surprising. Some people felt confined by a small town where everyone knew each other. Especially if that person was up to no good. Word got around quick about who to avoid and who to hang around with.

Reggie looked up from his plate. "I'm not the talkative type."

"Are you sure about that, Reggie?" Zach stated. "Because someone damaged a new resident's property and you are the only person around who has motive, considering your mother used to own the place and you have no other business in town."

Standing, Reggie glared at Zach.

Barstock made a move for his pocket.

"Hands where I can see 'em," Zach took a step back and rested his hand on the butt of his Glock.

Reggie put his hands in the air. "I was trying to pay my bill." His tone sounded bitter.

"Where is your wallet?" Zach drew his weapon and took another step away from Barstock.

The air in the diner thickened with tension.

Nate thought about the fact that his gun was in the truck. He had an open carry permit and kept a pistol in his truck at all times. It was meant to shoot pests on the ranch and was easier than carrying a shotgun, not to mention more accurate.

From where Nate sat, he could see Zach's finger hovering over the trigger mechanism of his department-issued weapon.

"My back pocket." The bitterness was gone from Reggie's voice, replaced by trepidation.

"Lower your right hand and use two fingers to pull it out. Keep your hand visible to me at all times,

Reggie. Do you understand?" Zach's commanding tone left no room for argument.

Nate had heard it used before and knew it was reserved for situations like this where Zach was uncertain of someone's motives. Not generally a good sign.

Nate glanced around, thinking he could take cover under the booth. He already knew where all the exits were, the one at the front door being the closest to him. He made eye contact with Liesel, who was frozen on the other side of the counter.

He nodded ever so slightly and she seemed to catch on. If the situation went south…duck.

Reggie did as commanded, pinching his wallet out of his back pocket.

"Keep your left hand in the air where I can see it," Zach demanded.

Now that Reggie had made an aggressive move, Zach had every right to take him to his office and interrogate him.

Reggie pulled out a twenty and tossed it on the table. He looked at Liesel. "That about cover it?"

"You're square with me," she said, her hands in the air, palms toward him.

"Hands on the counter," Zach said to Reggie in that authoritative-cop voice Nate had heard on the occasional ride-along.

"What did I do?" Reggie barked the question, but seemed to realize that his best move was to do as he was told.

"Keep your feet apart," Zach directed, wanting

to ensure Reggie wasn't a threat, which meant a pat-down to make certain the man wasn't carrying a weapon. He moved closer to Reggie, whose legs and hands were now planted wide.

"Look, man, all I'm doing is eating breakfast before I get back on the road," Reggie said.

"That your car in the parking lot?" Zach patted Reggie down as he asked.

"Yeah. So what?" Reggie quipped.

"Where are you headed tonight?" Zach finished the body search and straightened.

"I haven't decided," Reggie said.

"Did you pay anyone a visit while you were here?" Zach asked.

"That's none of your business," Reggie retorted.

"Everything that happens in my town is my business." Zach made sure of it. Especially since the hoof butchering had started and three years later there were still no leads. "You want to answer my question here or in my office?"

Reggie moved around the stool and Nate noticed the man had a slight limp. The hairs on the back of his neck prickled.

Zach had noticed it, too, based on the look he shot Nate.

"Did you do something to your left foot?" Zach's brow arched.

"It's my leg. It's nothing. Gout. I need to put it up." Reggie tried to blow it off, but Zach had zeroed in.

"You sure about that?" Zach asked. "Take five

steps." He motioned the opposite direction of where Zach stood.

Reggie limped along a few steps before grabbing onto the counter stool. "That far enough?"

"Yes, sir." Zach didn't have probable cause to arrest Reggie, so the man would have to show up at Zach's office of his own free will. "Did you make up your mind about staying in town tonight?"

"I've decided to keep driving. I was just passing through town and stopped off for a bite. Is there something illegal about that, Sheriff?" Reggie turned around, slowly, careful not to put too much pressure on his leg.

It was impossible to tell if he was favoring his left foot or his leg. It had already been established the person butchering the heifers walked with a limp.

Reggie's mother had left him out of her will. She owned a home and a site downtown that Chelsea was planning to use for a restaurant. Nate needed to ask her about other relatives being mentioned in the will. He hadn't thought to do that before. They'd been so focused on her ex being the one who'd thrown the rock. Could Maddie Barstock's son have done it?

It was a minor crime, at best. The stuff of juvenile delinquents.

"Before you take off, I'd like you to stop by my office to answer a few questions," Zach said.

"And if I don't?" Reggie was pushing his luck.

There were literally hundreds if not thousands of traffic laws in Texas that no one could possibly know about. All Zach needed was one, like anything mechanically to be broken on Reggie's car, for Zach to haul the guy in.

"I noticed you taking up two spots out there. One of which is for handicapped drivers," Zach stated.

"I'm barely on the line," Reggie said defensively.

"But on it," Zach said.

He and Reggie locked gazes and stared each other down for a long minute.

"All I need is one violation to impound your vehicle and hold you in my office. We're going to have a conversation whether you like it or not. So, we can do this the hard way or the easy way. One is going to cost you money. You decide." Zach had laid down the gauntlet. He'd holstered his weapon and let his hand rest on the butt of his gun.

Reggie finally put his head down and said, "Fine."

"You need the address?" Zach asked.

"I already know it." Reggie limped past Zach and toward the front door.

"Good. Then, I'll follow you." Zach walked a couple of steps behind Reggie.

Nate made eye contact with his cousin. "I'll bring food."

Zach thanked him and then followed close behind Reggie before closing the door.

Liesel blew out a breath once the men were outside. Nate didn't dare take his eyes off Reggie. He had a bad feeling about that man, that limp.

Questions swirled like a swarm of bees. Could this man, who lived out of town, have come back to visit his mother's vacant home or business during the times the animals had been butchered?

Other questions popped into Nate's mind, like how well his brother knew Reggie. Was it possible that someone in the Kent family had done something to the man to make him want to exact revenge? If that was the case, why maim animals? They were innocent.

There was Reggie's mother to consider. Had she cut her only son out of her will? It seemed so. There would have to be a story behind that decision. Chelsea would have answers, but she wouldn't be awake for a few more hours.

Thinking about her brought up the memory of the kiss they'd shared.

Nate stuffed that thought down deep where it belonged.

"DID HE START talking on the way over?" Nate asked Zach when he arrived at his cousin's office and set the bag of food on the desk.

"Quiet as a church mouse," Zach stated. "I'm letting him sweat it out in there now."

"He didn't ask for a lawyer?" Nate was curious how this scenario was going to play out. He was also thinking about Chelsea more than he wanted to admit. She'd invaded his thoughts multiple times on the ride over. He'd tried to convince himself that it was purely out of concern for the sweet family, for the fact that they were new in town. Nate had no idea what starting over was like. He'd been fortunate to have a solid foundation at the Kent ranch. He'd always had a roof over his head and plenty of food on the table. Nate never took that for granted. He'd never had to worry about putting a child to bed hungry. He was pretty certain that was at least part of the fear he'd seen in Chelsea's eyes a few hours ago. It had hit him square in the jaw.

Nate opened the bag on Zach's desk and handed him a container. "Can you arrest him?"

"Have no reason to," Zach stated as he took the foam box and opened it. He grabbed a packet of utensils and pulled out a napkin.

"Care to elaborate?" Nate asked, taking a seat in front of Zach's desk.

"There's no doubt in my mind that he's guilty of *something* but I have nothing to hold him on," Zach stated. "There are no witnesses and I have no evidence."

"Did Long lift any prints earlier?" Nate asked.

Zach shot his cousin a look. "You know I'm not technically allowed to discuss the details of the case with you."

"When will you know if there's a match?" Nate asked, figuring that ship had sailed a long time ago.

Zach took a bite of his BLT and then checked his watch. "Couple of hours."

Nate wanted to be the one to tell Chelsea the news. He'd be overstepping his bounds, but he wanted to give her the relief that her ex was most likely not responsible for what had happened. He could only hope it wasn't the case. Based on his estimation, Reggie Barstock was a solid suspect.

"Can I ask you a question?" Zach caught Nate's gaze.

Nate wondered if the question his cousin was about to ask had anything to do with Chelsea. "Go ahead."

"What's got you so interested in this case?" Zach took another bite of his BLT.

"I took the yesterday morning about her kid. Nice family," Nate said by way of explanation.

"Didn't say they weren't." Zach took another bite and chewed. "We have lots of nice families in Jacobstown. Does your interest in this one have anything to do with the beautiful *and single* blonde?"

Chapter Eight

"I wonder if Deacon remembers much about Reggie." Nate set the empty container next to the take-out bag on Zach's desk.

"You didn't answer my question." Zach's eyebrow shot up.

"There's nothing to comment about. I took a call that was a gut punch. You know how that is. A single mom moving to a new place in order to start over. Seems like these ladies have had a rough go lately and I can't help but think how fortunate we are for being grounded here in Jacobstown despite what we've been through with the heifers recently. You know?"

It was more than Nate had planned to say, but he figured Zach wasn't going to stop asking until he got some kind of answer—and that was as good a one Nate could think up. There was more of a pull to Chelsea than he wanted to acknowledge or to admit to, which was most likely why he'd left specifics about her out of his explanation.

Granted, it was none of Zach's business where

Nate spent his time, but the two had always enjoyed a close relationship and Nate had no reason to lie. Everything he'd said was true.

"Yeah, I know what you mean." Zach seemed willing to leave it at that. "I agree about asking your brother about Reggie. I saw that you picked up on his left foot giving him trouble."

"Might be nothing. Hell, ever since those incidences began, I've been on the lookout for anyone who favored his or her left foot after footprints confirmed a limp on that side," Nate admitted.

"Same here. We'd be stupid not to pay extra attention to anyone with a deformity or injury to the left side," Zach confirmed. "I've had my deputies scour through every document they could find for an injury that might be related. We tracked down a few names. I was especially looking for anyone who'd triggered an animal trap."

"You know we don't use those on our land," Nate said.

"No, but illegal hunters do."

Zach was stating a simple truth. As much as everyone on Kent Ranch worked to keep illegal hunters off the property, they couldn't keep all the criminals from getting close. Poaching was a lucrative industry. There would always be illegal hunters. Kids could be setting traps as some sort of cruel joke.

Nate nodded agreement. "What's the next move?"

"Dig into Reggie's background. If he has alibis for the dates in question, he's in the clear." Zach leaned back in his chair.

"I have a bad feeling about this guy. I just don't know how deep it goes yet," Nate admitted.

"Same here. He's up to no good. What do you know about the Barstock widow?" Zach opened a file on his computer.

"I know about as much as everyone else in town does. She kept to herself in her last years here in Jacobstown. I think the Rotary Club used to check on her and there are a couple of widows in town who put meals together for anyone who's sick or can't get out. I know that she moved away a couple of years ago. I'd forgotten she had a son, to be honest." Nate wasn't aware of any other next of kin and he certainly would've remembered Chelsea if she'd been in town before.

"The only good news is that this is the first possible lead we've had in the Jacobstown Hacker case." Nate hoped for resolution before the guy became bolder and moved on to humans like everyone had feared recently when a man in Fort Worth killed joggers by hacking off their foot and leaving them to bleed out. He'd been careless and had butchered the wrong foot. But copycats could multiply and no one would rest easy until the twisted jerk maiming animals was behind bars.

"I need to dig deeper into her background, too." Nate knew Zach was referring to Chelsea McGregor. "A stranger shows up in town and brings trouble."

"Her ex is here." Nate ignored Zach's look and kept right on talking. "He's worth investigating, if not for the rock then for the trouble it sounds like he might bring."

Zach was already rocking his head.

"I already have that in motion, too." He glanced at the notepad on his desk.

His cousin looked tired from the inside out. He'd been busy between the heifers' hooves being butchered and other crimes that had found their way to Jacobstown in recent weeks. Several of which had involved his brothers and their wives. Zach cared about every citizen in his jurisdiction. His family was no exception. The McWilliamses and Kents were a close-knit bunch.

"How's Amy, by the way?" Nate asked, referring to Zach's sister.

"She seems a little lost after graduating." Zach's shoulders slumped.

"Amber's been busy at the ranch," Nate said.

"Those two used to be joined at the hip and now Amy seems restless." Zach smiled but it didn't reach his eyes, his worry evidenced by the near constant lines bracketing his mouth. "She's trying to figure out her next move. I told her she should move to a bigger city, like Austin or San Antonio. She said she didn't want to leave Amber."

"They were the only two girls in a family of boys. Makes for a tight bond. You think there could be something else going on with her?"

"Good question," Nate said.

"Hey, at least our sisters can hold their own in

pretty much any situation." Zach laughed and the break in tension was a nice change.

Everyone at home, including Nate, had been on edge. It had started with their father's death and then the situation with the heifers had made it impossible to relax. There'd been more danger in town in the past couple of years than in Jacobstown's entire history. Good stuff had happened, too. It was all too easy to forget the good in times of strife. There'd also been marriages and babies. Several of Nate's siblings had found true happiness.

With Zach's recent reunion with a former girlfriend, Jillian Major, it was down to Nate and Jordon, the youngest brother, as the only bachelors left in the family.

"We haven't announced anything yet…" Zach glanced down at his phone. The wallpaper was a picture of Jillian touching her stomach.

"Are you telling me…?" Nate couldn't believe his ears. Stunned didn't begin to describe his feelings.

"We're having a baby." The love in Zach's eyes convinced Nate becoming a father was the logical next step for his cousin.

"It feels like you two just got back together."

Zach nodded and smiled. "I guess when you know, you know."

Nate had never experienced such a lightning bolt, but he'd heard tell of it from some of his siblings. They'd explained it was like a jolt out of nowhere and a sense of knowing they were in deep.

That annoying voice in the back of his head said

he'd been hit with something when he'd met Chelsea, but that was ridiculous. He didn't even know her. Jillian and Zach had grown up across the street from each other. They had history.

Then again, that explanation didn't exactly hold water because a couple of his brothers had met and fallen for the loves of their lives without knowing each other before.

"Congratulations, man. I couldn't be happier for you and Jillian." Nate gave his cousin another hug then stepped back.

"Where are you headed?" Zach asked when Nate didn't return to his chair.

"Grab a few hours of shut-eye before work starts. Keep me posted on Reggie, will you?"

Zach nodded. "Keep the part about the baby between you and me for now. She wants to surprise everyone by inviting them to a barbecue. She doesn't want a lot of formality. Just family and a few close friends out at the lake house we're building." Zach's face softened some of the hard worry lines when he spoke about his fiancée.

"You can count on me," Nate said.

Besides, Zach wasn't the only one with a secret.

CHELSEA FIGURED THE Dumpster behind the restaurant would be full by the end of the day. She needed about five more of them to properly clean this place out.

Work was good and she enjoyed the feeling of progress on her new restaurant. She'd also been careful to lock the door behind her so there were no surprises this time. The contractor who could knock out the walls where glass would be installed was due tomorrow bright and early.

She blew on her cold fingers to warm them. It must've been hovering around freezing outside and she refused to turn on the thermostat until she got closer to opening day. It was imperative to keep expenses down so she could have a successful grand opening. Starting out in a financial hole was not the way to kick off a business.

Soon enough, the place would be ready and the doors would open. Money would flow, or at least she hoped it would. Excitement came in the form of tingly sensations in her stomach. She was so ready for life to take a positive turn and for her to get back on track after being shoved off on the first go-round. She'd never expected a second chance and had no plans to waste the gift she'd been given.

Travis had been a temporary setback. She wouldn't allow him to rattle her the same way he had yesterday. For one, the element of surprise was no longer on his side. She'd let her guard down temporarily. No more. She would be ready if he popped up again. And she planned to buy pepper spray in case he brought a bad attitude with him when he showed.

During the multiple trips she'd taken to the Dumpster in the last few minutes, she'd checked both ways before exiting the building, like a young kid crossing the street for the first time. Luckily, there'd been no signs of Travis.

Chelsea locked the back door and walked into what would become her finished kitchen. A knock sounded at the front door. Her heart skipped a beat. The metal door hid the figure on the other side.

She considered not opening it.

Skylar was at school. Her mother was probably at the grocery store by now. Chelsea wasn't expecting a delivery. But then experience had taught her that didn't mean there wasn't one waiting on the other side of that door.

Taking in a sharp breath, Chelsea marched toward the door. The metal needed to go. She'd make a note to replace it with glass ASAP.

Another knock sounded, stopping her in her tracks.

"Chelsea." The familiar voice brought a wave of calmness over her. Nate Kent.

She couldn't get to the door fast enough.

"Come on in." She held it open.

"Sorry to interrupt." He glanced around as he stepped inside.

She closed and locked the door behind him.

"It's taking shape in here," Nate said.

"I still have a lot to do and not much time, but everything's on schedule so far." She couldn't afford to give up a day if she wanted to stick to her timetable.

Chelsea took an emotional hit seeing Nate again. She'd thought about the kiss they'd shared far too often for her own good last night.

Seriously, it was just a kiss. There was no need to get all weak-kneed just thinking about how impossibly soft his lips were for a face of such hard angles or how much better coffee tasted on them.

"There's coffee over there if you'd like a cup." She forced her gaze away from his mouth.

"You already have water?" he asked.

"I brought some with me." Nate looked just as good as he did last night. In fact, he looked almost exactly the same as he did last night.

"I don't mind a cup." He glanced around.

She pointed to the corner next to the new firebrick oven where she'd set up a small folding table and put coffee supplies on it.

"Water won't be turned on for three more weeks. I bring in a jug to make coffee." She had a couple of foam cups, too.

Nate poured a cup and took a sip. "It's good."

"It's the blend I plan to serve." His approval sent a burst of pride rushing through her.

"I met up with Zach last night to grab a bite after we left your place. Ran into someone unexpected. Are you aware that Mrs. Barstock's son is in town?" he asked.

"Um, no. Wow. I thought he'd moved out west somewhere. He wasn't invited to the reading of her will, so I guess I figured he didn't come around anymore." Chelsea was shocked to hear the news.

"He's driving a car with Louisiana plates," Nate mentioned.

"There's another surprise." She could've sworn the attorney had said Reggie had disappeared out west. "He doesn't have a right to the property or business. My great-aunt was clear about that and her lawyer assured me that I was the sole inheritor. Her will is iron-clad."

"How well did you know your great-aunt?"

"I didn't. This whole inheritance came out of the blue for me." She motioned to the fold-up chairs tucked underneath the table with the coffee. She needed to sit after hearing this news. The ground had shifted just a little. "According to her lawyer, Aunt Maddie had me tracked down after she fell and broke her hip. She knew her son would throw her money away and she wanted it to go to someone who would know what to do with it. She hit a bull's-eye there."

"Looks like she made the best choice."

Nate's compliment made her smile. "Thank you." She looked Nate in the eyes. "What did he want?"

"He didn't say. Tried to convince us that he was just driving through town in the middle of the night on his way home."

And then it dawned on her.

"The rock in my window. You think Reggie was trying to scare me?" She smacked her flat palm on the table.

"Or make a threat. Zach is trying to get more information out of him while he finds out if there's a clear print from the scene." Nate took another sip of coffee. A little liquid spot remained on his bottom lip.

Chelsea was transfixed by it.

"When will he know for sure?" This sure changed

things. Her initial reaction last night was that Travis had to have been involved with the rock throwing. Was it even possible he'd made his presence known then disappeared when he hadn't gotten what he'd wanted? Part of her hoped so. She never wanted to have to deal with him again for the rest of her life, and she had been clear about that.

If he came back and had a job and could show that he was responsible and ready to be a father, she'd consider allowing him to be part of Skylar's life. Anything less than that and Travis was just blowing hot air by talking to Chelsea. She wouldn't allow him around her daughter without a court order.

"Did Reggie seem upset?" she asked.

"You could say that. Have you ever met him?" Nate asked.

"No. I don't remember meeting my great-aunt, either, but my mother says I did when I was a kid." Chelsea ran her finger along the rim of her cup. "Her lawyer said she asked him to track me down. He apparently hired a PI to gain information about me. I guess Aunt Maddie was satisfied with what she saw. I did used to own and run a successful small business. Maybe that's why she thought I'd know what to do with her home and space.

"She must've also learned that the business's failure wasn't exactly my fault. I didn't mismanage the money. The business folding didn't have anything to do with me." Except, that part wasn't exactly truthful. Her business had failed because she'd trusted someone she shouldn't have. That part was very much on her.

"You must've made quite an impression." Nate focused on her finger rimming her cup and it sent a sensual shiver up his arm.

Chelsea's cell buzzed. Her heart skipped a beat as she jumped up and stalked toward the sound. She tracked it to where she'd left it on top of what would be a cabinet once it was hung.

"Hi, Mom," she answered with a glance toward Nate.

"Someone's in the house," her mother said.

Chapter Nine

"What do you mean? Like, *now*?" Chelsea's voice raised an octave as a look of panic washed over her.

Nate got to his feet and was by her side. She tilted the phone, giving him access so they could both listen.

"The back door stood wide open when I got here and I heard a noise upstairs, so I got out of there," Linda said.

"Thank heavens you're not still inside. Where are you now?" Chelsea asked.

"I'm in my car. I turned right around and walked out the door, got in my car and locked the doors." Linda sounded like a schoolkid who'd just shown her prize drawing to the class. "I figured this was the best place for me to call you."

"Stay where you are. I'm on my way," Chelsea said. "And don't hang up."

"I'll drive." Nate was already guiding Chelsea to the metal door leading outside, his hand at the curve of her back. It felt a little too natural for it to be there, a little too right. This close, he could smell her unique scent, a mix of wildflowers and dark roast coffee. It was fast becoming his favorite combination.

His truck was parked out front next to her pickup. He paused long enough for her to lock the door to her restaurant.

Chelsea rushed to the passenger side of his truck while he made a beeline for the driver's side. Normally, he'd open the door for her, but that courtesy would waste time and Linda had sounded scared.

The ride to her place on Sycamore took eight minutes, a record for cutting across town.

"We're almost home, Mom. Hold on a few more minutes for me, okay?" Chelsea shot a worried look at Nate.

On instinct, he reached out and touched her hand to comfort her. Those annoying jolts of electricity didn't seem to know when to let up because a few blasted his hand and vibrated up his arm.

Nate withdrew his hand and returned it to the steering wheel where his grip remained white-knuckled for the rest of the block. He pulled up next to Linda's parked sedan, essentially blocking her from the house. If someone charged out the front door, they'd have to get through Nate first.

"Call Zach," he said to Chelsea as he grabbed his pistol from underneath the bench seat. "Get your mother in my truck and lock the doors. Anything happens, I want the two of you to get out of here."

Chelsea started to argue but he was already dashing around the back of the house and out of earshot.

He hoped she would be smart enough to listen even though he got the feeling she wasn't used to stepping aside and letting someone else take charge.

In this case, she'd be crazy to follow him, and she didn't strike him as someone who would take an unnecessary risk.

Nate slowed at the kitchen door, his pistol pointed in the direction he walked. He had the butt of it secured in his grip and his finger hovered over the trigger. A bullet waited in the chamber.

There were two known possibilities. Reggie had most likely been released by now. Zach hadn't had a reason to keep the man locked up. He could've decided to take matters into his own hands. He'd grown up in this house and something of his might still be here. It was possible that he'd returned to take it back. Or, he wanted Chelsea out.

The other known quantity was her ex. He could be looking for their daughter, trying to catch Chelsea unaware. That possibility sat a little sour in Nate's gut. It wasn't his place to interfere with a family, but there was no way he'd stand aside and allow a man to intimidate his ex.

A burst of anger shot through him that he had no business allowing. Rational thought took over. Nate reasoned that Skylar's father wouldn't likely break in while no one was home. What would he have to gain?

Nate crossed the kitchen, careful not to step too hard on the wood floors. An ill-timed creak could end this day very badly.

The kitchen was eat-in. He made his way around the table with four chairs. A vase of fresh flowers on the kitchen table brightened up the place. Nate had a feeling that Chelsea could make any space feel like home in a matter of minutes. There was something warm about her that made him want to talk to her and tell her all his secrets. The feeling was foreign as hell. Nate wasn't a chatterbox. And he didn't *do* talking, much less about emotions. He'd never been this much inside his own head in his life.

He made his way through the door separating the kitchen from the living room. There was a guest room off the living room. He'd noticed the layout yesterday morning. It was habit to memorize a house's layout in case he ever had to come back for an emergency.

The door had been open and the bed pushed to one side. There were boxes stacked in that room in random order, too.

A siren wailed in the distance. Backup was on its way. Nate blew out a sigh of relief. He continued through the downstairs before checking the closet underneath the stairwell with the crawl space. He was familiar with that area, too, of course. The minute he opened the door, a cold gust of wind blasted him. Damn.

The sirens stopped right outside. Within a few seconds, a voice sounded from the kitchen. "I'm coming in."

It was Zach.

"I'm in the downstairs hallway," Nate shouted.

Zach had taught his cousin the protocol for hot situations long ago. Combine Zach's advice with Nate's volunteer firefighter training and he'd been told that he was handy to have around in an emergency.

A few seconds later, Zach was beside him.

"The bedroom hasn't been cleared and neither has the upstairs. The crawl space that I boarded up has been busted through," Nate informed his cousin.

"Okay. Good work. Are you ready to clear the rest of the house?" Zach would want to ensure no one was hiding in one of those rooms.

"Let's do it." Nate wouldn't be able to sleep without knowing the place was clear.

Side by side, they cleared each room. Nate checked the attic, just to make sure no one was hiding there. There were no basements in Texas to worry about, so once they cleared the upstairs, it was safe.

Nate followed his cousin outside to deliver the news to Chelsea and her mother. He let Zach take the lead.

"The place is clear. My deputy is on the way to see if he can lift prints off the door and the closet with the crawl space," Zach said.

Chelsea's gaze bounced from Zach to Nate. The terrified look in her eyes was a gut punch.

Zach briefed her as the same deputy from last night showed up.

"I'm sorry we didn't get a print yesterday. Maybe we'll get lucky this time," Deputy Long said before rounding the corner and getting to work.

"When he's finished, I'd like you to take a walk through the residence to see if anything's missing," Zach said to Chelsea.

"Half of our stuff is still in boxes." Chelsea sounded exacerbated. "How would I know?"

HAVING A SAFE home was important. Having the restaurant open on time was important. Having her sanity was important.

Chelsea saw her schedule blowing up before her eyes. It was shaping up to be a long day, and she couldn't afford to lose a day of progress at the restaurant.

The deputy finished his work quickly and a locksmith put a dead bolt on the back door as well as a new one on the front. It didn't hurt to ensure that Chelsea and her mother were the only key holders.

By lunch, Chelsea hadn't made it back to the restaurant. Nate had the closet patched up again in no time. Chelsea paid the locksmith from money she needed for the restaurant. She'd set the funds aside to buy tile floors. She'd have to go with painted concrete instead, a minor adjustment, but she was proud of herself for coming up with a contingency plan.

Reggie Barstock might be long gone. Zach had said the man had been released before the sun came up this morning. Chelsea guessed he could be responsible for the break-in. According to the sheriff, the lock had been jimmied. Chelsea had no idea what that entailed, except that it meant her new home had been easy to breach.

To Chelsea's thinking, Travis was up to something. Maybe he'd broken in to get information about her or his child. When it came to Travis, she knew to be suspicious. There'd been no sign of him, but that didn't mean he was gone. And how would he know where she lived? She guessed he could've asked someone. People would knew each other's business in a tight-knit community like Jacobstown.

Zach had promised to keep an eye out for her ex.

Wishing there'd be prints this time might be overly optimistic. The same person who threw the rock could be the one they were looking for now.

Chelsea was grateful that Skylar wasn't home to witness the break-in. She would never feel safe in the house. Anger pierced Chelsea. She *could* provide a safe home for her daughter, dammit. No one got to take that away from her.

By the time Chelsea got her mother settled and herself back to the restaurant, she only got in a half days' worth of work. She reminded herself that it was better than nothing. Surprisingly, Linda hadn't called more than twice and both times were in the first hour. Chelsea had texted her mother and was satisfied with the response she'd received stating that she was doing better knowing the place was locked.

Before she realized, it was time to pick up Skylar.

Chelsea was careful to make sure no one was parked out front near her pickup. She locked the metal door while checking side to side. No one would sneak up on her again, either. Her heart gave a little squeeze, reminding her that she missed Nate. A piece of her had hoped that he would stop by this afternoon.

Getting into her pickup, she locked the door behind her. She started the ignition and maneuvered onto the road leading to Skylar's school.

It was all good. Nate had a life on the ranch that he had to get back to. Shock didn't begin to describe her reaction to him owning the place. She was still trying to get over the fact. Using her phone, she'd looked him up last night and discovered that his family was one of the wealthiest ranching families in Texas. It struck her as odd that he was so well off.

Nate Kent was *one of* if not *the* most down-to-earth person she'd ever met. He'd mentioned that his parents were gone. She couldn't help but wish she'd been able to meet them. They'd done an excellent job with their children if the others were as grounded as him. Based on the couple of headlines she'd read, they were. They'd also been through a lot in the past few years and seemed to be stronger for it. With parenting skills like that, Chelsea wished she could ask questions.

Chelsea loved her own mother. Linda McGregor had been through the ringer and back. Her health was ailing. Chelsea couldn't help but feel responsible for her mother. Looking back, she couldn't remember a time when she hadn't felt like she needed to take care of the woman.

It was most likely the reason she felt so strongly

about making sure Skylar had as carefree a childhood as Chelsea could give her.

In the adult relationship department, Chelsea had
touched that stove. It was hot. She'd got burned. And
she was smart enough not to make the same mistake
twice. At least she hoped she'd learned from her er-
rors in judgment. The best way to take a hot pan off
a stove was to wear an oven mitt.

Thankfully, Chelsea was the second parent at
pickup. Skylar had noticed. The joy in her eyes made
the day Chelsea had had sting a lot less. There was
something magical about looking into her daughter's innocent eyes.

On the way home, they sang the song Skylar had
learned at school. What was it about singing with
her daughter that seemed to make the world's trou-
bles wash away?

"Hey, Momma, look," Skylar said as they pulled
up at home. Her daughter's voice had that excited
pitch usually reserved for a first peek at an un-
wrapped birthday present.

Chelsea saw Nate's truck parked on the pad. Her
first instinct was to panic. Her second was to check
her phone, which she did the second she pulled up
to the four-way stop sign. There were no stressful-
sounding texts or missed phone calls from her
mother.

Nate had boarded up the crawl space even better
the second time.

"What's the fireman doing here?" Skylar asked.
Another rogue wave of panic washed over Chel-

sea. Was her mother okay? Had something else happened? Chelsea scanned the windows and saw that everything was intact.

"Let's go see for ourselves," Chelsea said to her daughter. The little flip her stomach gave at the thought of seeing him again belied her calm façade.

She took her daughter by the hand and walked to the porch. The door swung open before Chelsea could reach for the knob.

Nate standing there in her house looked a little too right.

"How's my mother?" Chelsea immediately asked, ignoring the flip-flop routine going on in her stomach.

Nate stepped outside and closed the door behind him. "I need to talk to you about something important."

He must've seen the look of fright in her eyes because he quickly added, "Linda's doing great. It's not about her."

"Hey, Mr. Fireman." Skylar beamed up at him so hard her little body vibrated with joy.

"Hello, Ms. Skylar." He smiled back at her and Chelsea's heart melted a little bit more. She couldn't afford to let her emotions run wild when it came to the handsome Mr. Kent. She needed to get a grip. Past experience had taught her that she couldn't exactly trust her judgment when it came to men. They didn't stick around and she had no time for heartbreak.

"What do you need to discuss?" Chelsea shored up her strength, ignoring the goose bumps on her arms.

Skylar let loose of her mother's hand and grabbed Nate's. He smiled down at her but tension lines bracketed his mouth.

He motioned toward the tire swing in the yard. Chelsea caught on. He wanted to talk in private and they could use the swing as a distraction for Skylar. Again, the man was good with children, but she wouldn't let that fact cloud her judgment.

"Hey, sweetie. Want me to push you on the swing?" Chelsea bent down to eye level with her daughter.

Skylar's answer came in the form of her squealing before making a run for it.

"Be careful," Chelsea shouted to the back of the little girl's bouncy ringlets.

She and Nate took their time walking toward the side yard. Her body pinged with electric current with him this close, but she was determined to ignore it.

"I brought a friend over to meet you guys and I'd like him to stick around for a few days until all this...*stuff*...blows over." She got the feeling he'd wanted to use a different word but had thought better of it considering Skylar was within earshot.

"Okay. What are we talking about here?" The image of a burly, unshaved nightclub bouncer struck her.

"He's big—"

"Do you really think it's necessary? Skylar might not be comfortable with a strange man in the house," she quickly said.

"Rofert isn't a man. He's a dog." He put his hand up to stop her from interrupting. "He's a stray who found his way to our ranch last year. He's a New-foundland who showed up dehydrated and hungry, but we nursed him back to health. He loves children and I've never seen a more protective dog over the animals in the barn. He took on a coyote and came out on top when it tried to eat our barn cat."

"He sounds like a wonderful animal and I'm grateful for the thought," she hedged. "I'm not sure it's such a good idea for him to stay here. What if Skylar gets attached, and she will."

"She can always come visit him at the ranch. We can set it up that you're babysitting him for me while I work. It's not a lie." He'd thought of everything and she appreciated him for it.

But if the animal was as large as he said, afford-ing food might be a problem.

"We can get by without him for a few days until everything calms down here. I don't want you to feel pressured to take him and that's why I wanted to talk to you first before Skylar met him. I promised her that I'd bring over a pony and he's the closest thing I've got that'll fit in my truck. If you don't want him here, then he'll come home with me tonight."

Nate's pleading look made her almost instantly cave.

She didn't have the money for a security sys-tem. A dog the size of a pony seemed like a good compromise.

"I'd rest easier knowing the three of you are safe," he stated. "And he's well behaved. He won't chew up your furniture or make a mess on the rug. Besides, Linda's home alone all day and she could use the company as well as the protection. He's great with kids. Heaven knows we have plenty now at the family ranch."

Those were all valid points.

Maybe if Chelsea shopped around, she could squeeze dog food into the budget for a few days. Skylar would love having Rofert around and it might help her acclimate to the new house if she had a buddy.

Plus, knowing her mother was safe would go a long way toward giving Chelsea the time she needed to focus on her restaurant. "What kind of food does he eat?"

"He's on a special diet. Don't worry about food. I'll supply it."

A loaner dog that came with its own food?

There was no way Chelsea could pass that up.

"I only came up with the idea because you mentioned getting a puppy at some point. I figured you weren't averse to dogs. What do you think?" The look of apprehension on the big, strong cowboy's face was adorable. It was clear that he wasn't trying to overstep his bounds.

"You might have a hard time prying my daughter off your dog when it's time for him to go home." Chelsea appreciated the way Nate had handled this situation. It could've been a potential powder keg if the conversation had gone down in front of Sky or she thought the dog was a present.

The wide smile on Nate's face caused a burst of pride to fill her chest. She reminded herself that pride could be dangerous.

"She'd be welcome to come see him anytime. Plus, he might get comfortable here and not want to leave if it's agreeable to you," Nate remarked. The smile on his face was a little too sexy.

Chelsea had never heard of a Newfoundland before. She'd never had a dog before. She and her mother had had to live off the good graces of relatives for most of Chelsea's young life, and the best Chelsea ever got for a pet was feral kittens the time she lived in the country. They'd lived underneath the trailer of one of her relatives. She'd sneaked cans of tuna outside to lure them close to her where she'd pet them and pretend they were hers. She'd daydream about living in house of her own one day and having a house full of pets. That dream came before the reality of vet bills and food costs that she'd seen living with relatives and their pets.

"How do you want to break the news to the little nugget?" Nate asked, motioning toward Skylar.

"Let's take her inside and see how she reacts," Chelsea said.

Chapter Ten

Chelsea opened the door and stepped aside, allowing Skylar an opportunity to see Rofert. "This is Mr. Kent's dog and he wants us to babysit while he works long hours for the next week or two. What do you think, Sky?"

The little girl took one step inside the house, locked eyes on the massive canine loping toward her from the kitchen and squealed. That kid's scream rivaled any tight-budget horror movie noise.

"What's his name?" Skylar jump-clapped, hopped and took off toward the large animal. Rofert had a thick brown coat, the color of coffee. His large head held noble brown eyes and soft floppy ears.

"Rofert," Nate advised.

"Can I pet him?" Skylar remembered her manners at the last second, right before she launched herself at the dog's neck.

For a second, Chelsea prayed that the animal was as forgiving as Nate had said and wouldn't be spooked by the overzealous four-year-old. But the large animal tilted his head down and let Skylar hug him. His tail wagged along with half of his backside and she figured that had to be a good sign.

"Like I already said, he loves kids," Nate said. "She'll be fine."

Chelsea's mother appeared from the kitchen.

"I doubt anyone wants to stop what they're doing long enough to eat, but supper's ready." Her mother motioned at Skylar, who was giggling and hugging the neck of the dog.

"You weren't kidding. He really is the size of a pony," Chelsea said to Nate.

"Just wait until you get to clean up outside after he eats." Nate's humor was a welcome change from the tension Chelsea had been feeling. But that dog weighed more than she did and she didn't even want to think about the shovel she'd need to use to clean up after him. Nate was right, though. Having a dog around would give her the feeling of much-needed extra security. She'd sleep better at night knowing they had extra protection. And the way he took to Skylar, he'd most likely sleep in her room.

This house had four bedrooms. There was one downstairs, which Chelsea planned to convert into a home office. There was no need for a guest bedroom, considering the only living relative she knew about was Reggie, aside from her mother who had a bedroom upstairs. She wasn't likely to invite him to stay overnight, so there wasn't much need to keep it like it was.

The room had been the dustiest one in the house. Chelsea figured Aunt Maddie hadn't had many people over. Chelsea couldn't help but wonder why she'd been selected by her great-aunt. The lawyer had stated that Reggie had turned out to be a disappointment and he and his mother hadn't kept in touch. Reggie might be a disappointment, but was he a danger?

Chelsea forced her thoughts to something more productive. "Thanks for the loan, Nate. I'm pretty sure you just made Skylar's week. You've done too much for us already."

His face cracked into a broad smile.

"It's common for people to help each other in these parts," Nate said, like it was nothing. "Guess it comes from being ranchers and farmers. We've always had to band together to survive. It's in our DNA."

"We could use more of that in the world," she said. "Speaking of food... Would you like to stay for supper?"

"I'm afraid not. Sorry. I have plans," was all he said.

"Oh. Right. I don't want to keep you." Chelsea ushered him to the door, embarrassed. Of course a man like Nate Kent would have a date, maybe a girlfriend. No, she reasoned, he seemed too honest to kiss her if he was in a relationship with someone else.

She stopped before opening the door and turned around. "Skylar, tell Mr. Kent 'thank you' for thinking of us to take care of Rofert."

Before he could tell her it was no big deal, Skylar was there, wrapping her arms around his legs in her biggest hug.

"When I grow up, I want to be a fireman just like you," Skylar stated. It was her most heartfelt compliment.

"I think Rofert would like that," Nate said, patting her on the back. Chelsea took note of how much he tensed.

It was probably just his training that made him so good with kids and not that he believed her daughter was exceptional or there was a special connection between the two of them. Chelsea's heart squeezed anyway. Seeing a man who was so good with little ones was such a nice change of pace.

"We'll take good care of *your* dog," Chelsea said to Nate.

Skylar unpeeled herself from the man's legs, spun around and charged toward Rofert. He barked and the sound was so loud it nearly shook the walls.

"He'll do that if anyone tries to come in night or day," Nate reassured Chelsea.

"A person would have to be crazy to break into a house with a noise like that coming at them," she said.

Nate's smile sent another jolt of electricity shooting through her. It was probably for the best that he couldn't stay for dinner. She didn't need the distraction or the eventual heartache.

When he left and she closed the door behind him, a little sense of disappointment rolled through her, causing her shoulders to sag. She tried to con-

vince herself that it was the stress of the last couple of days.

Deep down, she knew it for the lie it was. Even
so, if she fell for the first guy who was nice and gave
her daughter a little positive attention, she might
as well pack up and go home. Only, she remembered that she had no home to go to. Jacobstown
was home. Maybe it would feel more like it when
the boxes were unpacked.

Chelsea joined her mother in the kitchen. "Smells
great in here."

"I cooked your favorite. Crispy beef tacos," Linda
said. "Figured we should celebrate our new beginning."

"Thank you, Mom." The woman always had the
sweetest of intentions. She'd done the best she could
bringing up Chelsea alone. Her mother deserved
better than what Chelsea had been able to give in
the past few years. She wanted to do better by her
mother. "I'll get Skylar."

The three of them ate at the kitchen table, chatting about their days. Rofert positioned himself on
the floor next to Skylar.

After dinner, the nighttime routine of cleaning
dishes, giving Skylar a bath and reading a bedtime
story kept Chelsea busy. Rofert stayed by Skylar's
side, which posed a problem in the small bathroom.
Chelsea had made it work. She was grateful for such
a loyal companion and she'd never seen a bigger
smile plastered on Skylar's face. Giving him back
was going to be difficult, but Chelsea promised her-

self that she'd figure out a way to get Skylar a puppy as soon as she could.

Rofert loped into Skylar's bedroom at lights-out. The house was perfect with three bedrooms upstairs along with a small landing. The master bedroom was at the top of the stairs and Skylar's room was next door. Some people might not prefer to have their children so close. It was an absolute necessity for Chelsea.

The rooms were small but cozy and the entire upstairs shared a bathroom. And it was perfect.

Rofert slept with his head half in the hallway. The big, hairy dog comforted Chelsea and she was even more grateful for Nate's thoughtfulness.

Her mother had retired to her room to read and Chelsea took a long, hot bath. She went to her room and dropped down on the bed, too tired to take her bathrobe off. Instead, she curled up under the covers and fell into a deep sleep.

In the morning, she'd half expected to walk downstairs to find Nate Kent in her kitchen. She hid her disappointment when it was her mother stirring around in there.

"I'm making pancakes," Linda said proudly.

"Since when did you become such a great cook?" Chelsea teased. There hadn't been many home-cooked meals growing up. Her mother had been too tired to cook after being on her feet all day working odd jobs as they'd come along.

"I take after my daughter." Linda winked.

"I'm afraid she might be a one-trick pony." Chelsea made her way over to the coffee machine. Fresh coffee smelled like heaven. Skylar would be up in another half hour. Chelsea cherished her morning quiet time before the day got into full swing. She poured the steaming liquid into a cup and headed for the back door.

"Rofert still snoring at Skylar's feet?" her mother asked.

"Yep." It was going to be hard to separate those two when the time came. She'd offer to keep him if it wouldn't cost a month of groceries to feed him for a week.

Chelsea slipped on a pair of sneakers, unlocked the door and pushed open the screen door. She looked out onto the third-of-an-acre lot. There was room for Skylar to stretch her legs out here. Chelsea took in a deep breath and then exhaled. A rogue tear escaped at the thought this belonged to Chelsea. She could make a home for her daughter here. She could provide a stable place for her mother to live.

It was cold outside but Chelsea didn't care. She wiped away the tear and headed to the mailbox at the end of the gravel lane.

"How's the restaurant going?" a voice called out from her left. "I'm Gayle Swanson, by the way."

Gayle Swanson was a woman in her late sixties to early seventies. She wore a hot-pink and black jogging suit. Her head was covered in gray hair in one of those shorter, flattering cuts. Her face was filled with smile lines.

"I'm Chelsea McGregor." Chelsea walked to the

chain-link fence and offered a handshake. The older woman had a surprisingly strong grip. She hoped this might be a friend for her mother. Linda needed more than Chelsea and Skylar. Her mother needed more to look forward to in life than helping take care of them. "It's nice to meet you."

"You getting settled in all right?" Ms. Swanson asked. "I'm not normally nosy, but it seems like there's been an unusual amount of excitement and I haven't had a next-door neighbor in years."

"We had some surprises at first, but everything is settling in all right now. Somehow a rock made it through that window." She pointed to the east living room window. "And someone broke in, but my mother interrupted them coming home from the grocery."

Gayle gasped. "That's awful. I'm sure sorry that's been happening. I saw that no-good Barstock boy around lately. I wondered if something was up. His mother and I go way back." She gave a pensive look. "She was older than me, so I kept an eye out for her in her last years at the house. I figured something must've happened to her when I saw the moving truck."

Chelsea nodded sympathetically.

"She said she had a beautiful great-niece who she would leave her home and business to one day. She must've been talking about you," Gayle observed with a point of her finger.

It was nice to speak to someone who knew her great-aunt personally. Chelsea's mother had no memories of Aunt Maddie to share. "I'm afraid I didn't know my great-aunt very well. This has all been a pleasant surprise. Did she say why she felt I was the right person to live here?"

"Said you were honest and hard-working. She saw a lot of herself in you."

Chelsea's chest swelled with pride. She thanked Gayle for telling her. "Did you also say that you saw Reggie around lately?"

"Mmm-hmm," she said with a begrudging look. "I don't know what happened to that boy. His mother was a saint for putting up with him as much as she did. She knew giving him the house and the store was out of the question. He'd sell 'em both bit by bit and blow the money gambling. He got mixed up with betting and got himself in some trouble. That's about all I know. Maddie didn't like talking about him. Said talk couldn't change a person and she'd tried everything in the book to set him right."

"I'm sorry." Chelsea'd had it rough and so had her mother, but neither would consider doing anything illegal. Travis hadn't technically stolen since he'd convinced her to put his name on the accounts. What he'd done was unconscionable and immoral, but not illegal.

"Well, you do what you can with your children and then you have to hope for the best," the older woman declared.

Chelsea liked Gayle. The woman had spunk. Her no-nonsense attitude was refreshing.

"Reggie's nothing like that Kent boy who's been

coming around. Remind me, which one is the fire-fighter?" Gayle asked and there was a twinkle in her eye.

"Nate," Chelsea returned. It was impossible to hide the flush in her cheeks when she thought about him. "And, yeah, he's been helpful. My daughter pulled something and ended up getting herself stuck in a crawl space. Luckily, she had my phone and was able to call for help."

"She sounds smart as a whip," Gayle declared with a girl-power-fueled fist pump.

Chelsea smiled. "Maybe a little too smart for her own good sometimes."

"A girl can never be too smart…or too rich," Gayle quipped.

"I wouldn't mind more of that last part," Chelsea joked.

"Has that Nate been coming around a lot?"

The question surprised Chelsea.

"A few days ago, when we were having some trouble, but not now." Chelsea stuffed down her disappointment.

"He's a catch, that one. But then, from what I've heard, he's not the 'settling down' type. He'll go out with this one for a week and that one the next. He's easy on the eyes. I don't think I've ever seen him with the same woman twice." She held up a finger and wagged it. "Well, that's not true. I'm a liar. He was going with one for a few months. She got transferred with her job and that was that."

"Oh. Well. I better get back inside. My daughter's due to be awake any minute and my coffee's gone cold." Chelsea didn't like hearing gossip about Nate. Even worse if it was true. He'd tensed up the other day when Skylar had grabbed onto his legs for a hug. Now it made sense why. If Gayle could be believed, he never stuck around one place for long and he'd probably moved on from Chelsea in the same manner. Why did that feel like a physical blow? What Nate Kent did with his personal life was none of Chelsea's business.

"Nice meeting you," Gayle said. "Can't wait for your grand opening. It's about time we got a new place to eat in town."

"Thanks. I look forward to seeing you at the restaurant." Chelsea turned away to hide the embarrassment heating her cheeks. She'd been thinking about the kiss she'd shared with Nate far too much and a silly part of her thought he might actually be attracted to her. He was just being nice. Granted, that didn't explain the kiss. Although it could've just been for curiosity's sake.

She stalked in through the back door and was greeted by the warmest sight. Skylar's arms wrapped around the Rofert's neck. She'd thrown her leg over his back and was hopping on one foot down the hallway, coming toward the kitchen.

When Chelsea really looked, she could've sworn that dog was smiling, too.

"How was your walk?" her mother asked.

"Fine. Cold." Chelsea moved to the coffeemaker and poured a second cup. She set the mug on the counter and bent down to greet her daughter. "Good morning."

Rofert's tail swished back and forth, nailing the fridge. He was a beautiful animal even if he did shed like crazy. When that big face with those serious brown eyes looked up at her, she bent and kissed him on the forehead. She didn't care about Nate Kent's motives or lack thereof. She appreciated his kindness and that's as far as she could let her feelings go.

The next few days were a blur of early mornings and long, productive days at the restaurant. The quiet was a welcome change from the excitement of the first few days in town. Except that Chelsea hadn't seen or heard from Nate. Much to her surprise, she missed talking to him.

There were other, darker issues lurking. She had no idea when and if Reggie Barstock would turn up again. Travis hadn't made himself known, either.

It was probably too much to hope the two of them would leave her alone and go about their own business. A creepy feeling that she couldn't shake made her fear that neither would walk away so easily. It was too quiet, like the calm before a raging storm.

She pushed those unproductive thoughts aside. Life was getting back on track. Her little family of three, plus Rofert, was starting to get into a good rhythm.

The restaurant still looked like a construction site but the floors had been cleared of debris. There were no more stacks of half-broken and dirty bricks littering the space. An open concept was perfect for the restaurant and made for easier renovations. A contractor had built a wall inside with a swinging door for the cleanup area so dirty dishes wouldn't be visible from the main cooking and dining area.

A lot of work still needed to be done, but damn if progress didn't feel amazing. Chelsea had noticed that progress was everything. The destination was sweet, and every inch of progress toward a clear vision sometimes felt like she was already there.

Aunt Maddie had been a business owner and Chelsea felt a connection to her great-aunt through their entrepreneurial bond.

She tried not to think about the fact that it was Saturday night and she was alone working in her restaurant. She hadn't once given a thought to working weekends. What was going on with her lately?

Nate Kent, that little voice in the back of her head pointed out.

It was an annoying little brat.

THE CALL CAME over the emergency response radio at one fifty-five in the morning.

"Fire at 2312 Main. All emergency personnel to respond."

Nate scrambled out of bed and threw on his ready outfit of jeans and a pullover shirt that he kept draped over the chair next to his bed. He hopped on one foot trying to slip a sock on. While he was on his second sock, a bolt shot through him—2312 Main Street was the address of Chelsea's restaurant!

It was the middle of the night. Surely she was home sleeping in her bed, he reasoned.

The dispatch continued. *"A pickup with license plate BZWG 1234 is parked in front of the building. An unknown number of occupants is inside the building."*

Nate hopped into his boots, grabbed his cell and broke into a dead run toward his truck. He raked his fingers through his curls in an attempt to tame them. His truck was parked in the garage, keys in the ignition. He kept a bottle of mouthwash in the cup holder for just such occasions.

On the road, Nate took a swig of the mouthwash, rinsed and then opened the window to spit while at the four-way stop. Everything about this call was routine except that his gut was braided in a tight knot at the realization Chelsea could be in the restaurant, hurt.

He'd left her and her sweet family alone to avoid just that: anyone getting hurt. But the kiss they'd shared had burned its way into his thoughts and popped up at the most inopportune times. He'd finally returned Brenda Hunt's call and agreed to a date to prove to himself that he could go out with someone and be fine.

The date had lasted half an hour before Brenda looked him square in the eye and asked, "Do you really want to be here?"

An honest question like that deserved a real answer. He'd spared her the "It's me, not you" line even though in this case it was true. Brenda was an attractive brunette. There was no reason he shouldn't have enjoyed her company. But the comparisons had crept in. All that date had told him was that he needed to spend some time alone.

The ranch had been keeping him busy and he enjoyed the long days and hard work. Calves were due to be born in a matter of weeks and keeping watch over the heifers gave him a sense of purpose.

Nate gunned the engine, pushing his truck to its limit, lights on. His rotating beacon drew circles against quiet street after quiet street. His pulse had shot through the roof and all he could think about was Chelsea.

Even in the dark, he could see the thick cloud of smoke. The flames licking toward the sky.

Fires were indiscriminate creatures that took on a life of their own.

They didn't care about the wreckage left behind. There were no feelings in a fire. They didn't care if they made widows and orphans.

Skylar's sweet face popped into his thoughts.

And then Chelsea's.

A sense of foreboding crept over him as he neared the scene. A fire truck had just arrived, based on the sound of the siren. Confirmation came on the radio a few seconds later.

Nate parked alongside the fire truck and bolted for the rig. He had his equipment on in a matter of minutes.

Details were being given over the radio but there wasn't much other than the severity of the blaze.

A crew was working the hose, twisting off the fire

hydrant cap at the corner and working quickly and efficiently to clamp on the hose. They had a steady spray going by the time Nate located his captain.

Nate already had his ax ready to go as he approached Steve Benton. "I'm ready to go in as soon as word comes."

"What's your rush?" Captain Benton asked.

"Chelsea McGregor is inside." His voice was calm although he felt anything but.

"How can you be certain?" Benton asked.

"That's her pickup. It would be just like her to pull an all-nighter to get back on schedule."

"She might've gotten a ride home with someone. I'm not sending a man in there until I know it's safe," his captain said.

Nate blew out a sharp breath. "I know her. She's in there. She has a daughter who needs her. If me going in means the difference between life and death for her, I'm willing to take the risk. I signed up for this job and I knew what I was doing." Nate was emphatic.

Captain Benton studied him carefully. "As soon as I give the all-clear, you'll be the first to go in. Right now we have a two-alarm fire and one engine to deal with it. The backdraft could take you and several others out if we tamper—"

"Like I said, I'm aware of the risks and I didn't ask anyone to come inside with me." Nate stood his ground. "I'm going in."

Chapter Eleven

Chelsea heard a voice in the distance but she couldn't move, couldn't respond. If only she could open her eyes... *Nate?*

It was probably wishful thinking that had her hearing his voice. She wished he was there, wished she could see him. She'd thought about him more than she cared to admit while she'd worked. His deep timbre normally washed over her, stirring a physical reaction. This time, he sounded concerned, and her body had a different kind of reaction to him. It went on full alert.

She wanted to shout to him, to tell him where she was, to stop him from being concerned about her. There was so much noise drowning him out. Crackling and popping.

Chelsea took in a breath and choked on it. She coughed. Everything burned; her eyes, her nose, her throat. Her lungs clawed for oxygen but came up short.

Out of seemingly nowhere something was being placed on her face. Then someone's arms lifted her like she weighed nothing. And then she took in a breath of air. She coughed like she'd just chugged water after being lost in the desert. Her lungs ached.

Time passed, Chelsea couldn't be sure how much before she finally took in a real breath. She heard several male voices telling her to stay awake. All she wanted to do was to sleep. She fought the urge.

"Skylar needs you," Nate said, his voice like a whisper in her ear.

Skylar's image popped into Chelsea's thoughts. She had to stay awake so she could get home to her daughter. Chelsea locked on to the thought.

By the time she could blink her eyes open, she was in the emergency room. Breathing still hurt and a headache threatened to split her head in two.

She forced her eyes to open and stay that way.

There he was, standing by her side, holding her hand.

"Nate—" Trying to speak caused a coughing jag.

"I'm here." He bent next to her bed while a nurse called for the doctor.

"Well, hello," the nurse said. "My name's Willow. I'll be taking care of you tonight."

Chelsea shook her head. She needed to get home. If word got home about the fire…*damn*, her restaurant had just gone up in flames. She'd cry if she could squeeze out a tear. Instead, she just felt deflated and drained of energy.

"It'll be okay," Nate reassured her, but he was wrong. Nothing was okay. Her livelihood had just gone up in flames. She'd been shopping around for insurance but hadn't settled on a company yet. Her to-do list was scary long. She'd been making progress, knocking off item after item.

And now this. *This.*

"Don't worry. Everything will work out." Nate squeezed her hand, causing all kinds of inappropriate volts of electricity to rocket through her. All she could think about was her mother and Skylar. How would Chelsea support the two most important people in her life now? That little voice tried to point out that Nate felt pretty darn important. She quashed the thought before it could gather steam and fought to stay conscious. There was something else niggling away at the edge of her consciousness. *What?*

Working all night at the restaurant by herself to make up for lost time was a mistake. It had left her vulnerable and almost cost her life. She couldn't imagine the fire had been an accident. If it had been set on purpose, who was to blame? This stunt went beyond trying to scare her. Her truck had been parked outside the restaurant. Was someone seriously after her? Had someone been watching her? Waiting for an opportunity?

Chelsea said a silent thank you for the fact the fire had been lit at the restaurant instead of at her home because it spared her mother and daughter.

"What were you doing there so late?" Nate asked.

"I'm so behind. I was trying to catch up." She squeezed her eyes shut trying to block the roaring headache forming between her eyes.

He must've been paying close attention and reading the signs because he quietly said, "Try to rest. I'm here. I'm not going anywhere."

For the next few hours, hospital staff came and went, asking questions and marking charts. Chelsea managed to sit upright and sip water on her own. Her eyes, nose and throat still burned, but her lungs ached less.

Dr. Newman was the on-call physician. He was a squatty-looking man with a ruddy complexion and easy bedside manner.

"You're lucky this man arrived when he did," Dr. Newman told her. "You took a fall that most likely knocked you out."

"That explains the horrible pounding going on back there." She gestured to her crown after lifting her oxygen mask. She already knew that she'd taken a blow to the head and that Nate had probably defied orders and probably good judgment when he'd burst through the back door. He'd gotten to her before she'd succumbed to smoke inhalation.

"We were lucky," Nate noted.

Chelsea would have to take the doctor's word on falling. Her memory was fuzzy. She didn't remember tripping or hitting her head. Now that she thought about it, she did remember hearing a voice and, for some reason, she thought she'd heard it before losing consciousness. A chill raced down her back.

She probably just had it mixed up with Nate's or an EMT's.

"Good news is that you can leave as soon as that

drip finishes." Dr. Newman motioned toward her IV bag. "But you have to put your oxygen mask back on a little while longer."

Chelsea replaced the mask.

"We'll get you out of here before you know it," Dr. Newman said.

She liked the sound of that. She smiled at Nate and her heart performed that freefall routine whenever he was near. She'd missed him the last few days. She'd missed the comfortable way she had with him. Even from the start, and forget the fact that they were strangers, she'd felt at ease talking to him. Granted, her body reminded her he was very much male and she was all female every time the two of them were in the same room. But even with all that sexual chemistry pinging between them, conversation with him flowed effortlessly.

"Any chance you'll let me give you a ride home later?" he asked.

It was either that or wake her mother up in the wee hours of the morning, who would, in turn, wake her daughter, and then come to pick Chelsea up from the ER. She was certain one of those ride-hailing services used in the city hadn't made it out to these parts. Ordering a ride would be impossible and, since she knew only one person in town other than Nate, so far...

"I'd appreciate that. Thank you," she said, lifting her mask to speak. "The more I think about what happened, the more I could swear I heard a male voice *before* I blacked out."

"Head injuries can be tricky. Are you sure about that?"

"Not absolutely certain. And yet, that's what I'm remembering."

CHELSEA LEANED HER head back on the passenger seat of Nate's truck. An hour had passed since the IV ran dry.

"Zach will stop by in a little while to get your statement. Make sure he knows about the voice," Nate stated. She could almost hear the wheels churning in his mind.

"That fire wasn't my fault. I didn't do anything for it to start. I keep racking my brain for something…a kerosene lamp…*something* that could've started it. I didn't so much as bring a space heater. I was cold while I worked but being inside kept the winds from freezing me. I was saving money on heat, so I had the thermostat so low I had to work in my coat and gloves." She was probably going to catch the death of a cold because of it.

Nate's forehead creased with worry lines. He white-knuckled the steering wheel. "Did you say the male voice sounded familiar?"

"Yes. But thinking back, I couldn't tell you who it belonged to." Her mind started clicking. "I can't even be certain I'm remembering correctly except that it feels like I am."

"Do you know what Reggie's voice sounds like? No one's seen him around town but that doesn't mean he's not here," Nate said after a thoughtful pause.

"No. What would he have to gain if the restaurant is destroyed?" He'd come to her mind, too. But she hadn't worked out a motive yet or where she might've heard his voice.

"He might want to scare you or run you out of town. Any word from the lawyer on who gets the home and the property if something happens to you?" he asked.

"Aunt Maddie didn't say. But isn't that obvious? I mean, even to a man like Reggie? I own the properties now. They'd go to my next of kin," she stated.

"He might think he'd have a better court case if you weren't in the picture. Or maybe he thinks you'll abandon the properties and then he can make a play for them." There was another option that he wasn't stating.

"Or he could just hate me for being the one she left everything to and want revenge."

Nate nodded as his gaze intensified on the road ahead.

"I'll call Zach and ask if he can come right over. The fire marshal will investigate the fire as part of insurance requirements before payout. I'll see if we can put some pressure on the investigation and get a verdict sooner."

"What if I don't have insurance?" She pinched the bridge of her nose to stave off a threatening headache. "I was still trying to decide which company to go with."

"There might be an umbrella policy from your aunt. We'll check into it," he said to reassure her.

She sat there, trying to make sense of what had happened. Details were fuzzy. She wished she could pinpoint who the male voice had belonged to.

The back of her skull had a knot on it.

"My purse and my cell are back at the restaurant." She hadn't seen them since the fire.

"I know this sounds cliché and it might not be what you want to hear right now, but all those things can be replaced."

"You're right," she said as he pulled into the drive.

"No one called your mother because we didn't want her to worry." He pulled up next to the house and parked.

"It's better coming from me."

A car was parked in the drive, causing Chelsea's pulse to skyrocket.

"It's Deputy Long. Zach sent him over to keep watch as soon as he heard about the fire," Nate stated. "He didn't want to take a chance with your mother and Skylar."

"What if it's my ex who started the fire. What if it's Travis?" she asked as she put her hand on the handle.

"What would he have to gain?" Nate gripped the steering wheel.

"My daughter." Travis had the most to gain if something happened to Chelsea. A wave of nausea nearly doubled her over.

She squinted through blurry eyes as she realized he was watching her.

"Let's get inside and get you in bed. Food will go a long way toward making you feel better," Nate said. His eyebrows were drawn together with concern.

Chelsea pushed open the door before he could get out and do it for her. He was at the passenger door before she could step out of the truck. She accepted his hand and then climbed out of the cab.

The sun was almost up. The lights flipped on in the kitchen. Her mother was awake. Thankfully, she was home and could explain everything before Linda worked herself up with too much worry.

Nate offered his arm and she took it, leaning much of her weight on him while ignoring the frissons of electricity pinging between them.

Linda was in the kitchen when Chelsea knocked on the back door. She swished the curtain over the top glass, saw Chelsea standing there with Nate, and immediately unlocked the door.

"What happened?" her mother asked.

Nate helped Chelsea to the kitchen table where she eased onto the chair.

"The good news is that I'm fine. The restaurant caught fire last night." Chelsea did her best to hide her emotions. Breaking down would only make things worse. Somehow, Chelsea would figure out a way to get the restaurant back on track. And hadn't she always been the strong one?

"I'm sorry, dear. You've been working so hard

and I know how much the place means to you." Her mother's concern was genuine. It was odd for Linda to be trying to comfort Chelsea when normally it was the other way around. "If I know my daughter, and I do, you'll figure out how to fix it and make it even better than it was before."

A rogue tear slipped down Chelsea's cheek as she embraced her mother.

Nate busied himself making coffee and she appreciated him giving her space to talk to her mother.

Rofert barked from upstairs and she'd never seen a person move as fast as Nate to reach him.

Chelsea pushed to her feet and did her best to keep up. She didn't want Skylar waking up to a stranger. That bratty voice in the back of her head reminded her that Skylar was well acquainted with Nate. The little girl had asked for the fireman more than once in the past few days.

Chelsea had been able to distract her by bringing up the one male figure who could be counted on, Santa Claus.

Taking the steps three at a clip, Nate was at the top of the stairwell in no time. Chelsea's lungs burned and she had to stop and grip the rail, which slowed her down considerably.

Rofert barked again from inside Skylar's room.

Why was the door shut?

By the time Chelsea made it to the top of the stairs, Skylar was lying full-out on top of Rofert who was on his side.

"What happened?" Chelsea asked, out of breath.

"The door was closed and I'm guessing Rofert heard us downstairs. He must not have realized who we were," Nate explained.

"It's my fault," her mother called upstairs. "I'm the one who closed the door so I could get some sleep from all that snoring."

Chelsea leaned against the wall and slid onto the floor. All the stress she'd been under and now the fire collided in a perfect storm of crazy. No one could predict any of the things that had happened, were still happening.

As far as she could tell, there were two options. Laugh or cry.

She laughed to the point of tears.

Chapter Twelve

Nate listened as Chelsea recounted everything she remembered to Zach. Her first lucky break was his cousin finding and returning her cell phone and handbag intact. Somehow those had managed to make it out of the fire undamaged. It was a miracle and would save her time and hassle by not having to replace her ID, credit cards and whatever else she kept in her bag.

The first thing she'd done was dig inside her purse. She palmed what looked like a photo. The look of relief on her face caught Nate off guard at first. She'd gone for the photo without checking her wallet.

According to her, her whole life was practically stored inside her handbag. Based on Nate's knowledge of his sister and cousin, Amy, that was probably true.

Linda had volunteered to take Skylar to school and Zach had sent Deputy Long to follow them, just in case. This wasn't the warm welcome most folks got when they came to Jacobstown.

The attack at the restaurant was bold. Someone had gotten into the place undetected while she'd worked. To the best of her knowledge, Chelsea'd sworn that she'd locked the front and back door.

That part was unsettling to Nate.

Could someone have a key? That brought his thoughts back to Reggie. In fact, most roads led to that jerk. Nate's hands fisted thinking about Barstock. He'd worn a smirk that didn't sit well with Nate.

The fire marshal wouldn't complete his report for a few days. They'd know then if the fire had been started from inside or out.

Chelsea had also brought up her ex, Travis.

Nate would be remiss to rule Travis out as a suspect.

"Travis said he's been working for a pipeline in Alaska trying to earn enough money to win us back," Chelsea told Zach. "I haven't had time to check out his story and I've been relieved that it was quiet for the past week."

Nate had forced himself to stay away from the little family of three. He'd busied himself on the ranch. It seemed like there was always something to fix or clean out back home.

"I can run a check on him with his legal name and social security if you still have it," Zach offered.

"It's in here." She dug through her bag and fished out a wallet. She pilfered through it until she produced a social security card. "It was tucked in my wallet years ago from before he left. He'd asked me to hold on to it and must've forgotten he gave it to me. I kept it just in case I needed it. There you go."

Zach snapped a picture of the card. "Did he mention where he might be headed next?"

"Actually, he was pretty insistent that he intended to stick around this time," she reported. Her face twisted in a look of disgust. Her feelings for her ex were strong and Nate didn't blame her. Any man who would clean out bank accounts and disappear while his wife was in labor was a class-A jerk and didn't deserve a second chance unless he moved mountains to get it.

Nate would never treat Chelsea like that if the two of them were married.

He almost choked on the thought of marriage. Suddenly, his collar was too tight. He tucked his finger inside the top button and tugged to loosen it.

Chelsea must've yawned four times in a row. Zach stood and made eye contact with Nate.

"I'll see him out," Nate said to her.

"Great. I need a hot shower more than I need air right now."

Chelsea didn't need to go putting images of her naked in his mind. He'd thought about that kiss more then was good for either one of them. In fact, that kiss was a large part of the reason he'd kept his distance.

But she was in trouble and he couldn't turn his back while she was in danger. Someone was targeting her. And the jerk seemed ready to do just about anything to make sure she stayed out of the way.

Nate walked Zach out the front door and stopped on the porch.

"You sticking around?" Zach asked.

"Yeah, why?" Nate must've sounded pretty damn defensive based on the look he got from his cousin, raised eyebrow included.

"Hey." Zach's hands rose in the surrender position. "I'm just trying to see what kind of manpower I need over here to make sure this family is safe. If you're sticking around, I can use my resources elsewhere on the investigation and less on a protection detail. That's all."

"Got it. Didn't mean to overreact," Nate clarified.

"No problem. I'm glad you'll be around. These three seem like good people and they look like they could use a friend," Zach continued.

Nate nodded agreement. "I'll give you a call if she remembers anything else."

"It's possible. Her brain could be blocking out the attack. Or, as her injury indicates, someone approached her from behind," Zach stated.

"Who else has a key?"

"I'm not sure. She could've left one of the doors unlocked." Zach looked away from the bright morning sun.

It was cold outside but the sun shining made a world of difference.

"Christmas is in a couple of weeks. Her ex might be getting sentimental about having his family back." Nate was thinking out loud.

"True. I thought about that possibility. She could've been killed in the fire."

"He might've been watching from somewhere, even planning to play the big hero and save her once the blaze hit fever pitch," Nate suggested.

"A twisted mind could think that, even if she died, a judge would grant him custody of his daughter and he'd get everything that little girl inherited." Zach rubbed the scruff on his chin. "I'll dig around in his background some more. Figure out where this guy's been during the last four years."

"Any word about Reggie's background?" Before Zach could play the I-can't-tell-you card, Nate put a hand up. "He's a relative of hers and if I'm going to stay here, I'd like to know what I could be dealing with. We both noticed him favoring his left foot."

"He's been brought in a few times in the past ten years for petty crimes. The best I can tell, he works odd jobs. Nothing seems to stick, according to Chief Smith in Bossier Parish. I called in a favor to find out that Reggie's been on the chief's watch list for several crimes." Zach's and Nate's cell phones went off at almost the exact same time.

They locked gazes for a split second before each taking a call.

"What's going on, Deacon?" Deacon was brother number three in the Kent hierarchy and the next closest to Nate in age.

"I haven't seen you much lately and I just heard a rumor about Reggie Barstock and a bad left foot…"

Deacon started. "Any possible connection to what's been going on at the ranch?"

"I'm at Chelsea McGregor's house talking to Zach about that right now," Nate admitted.

"I don't have to tell you the longer we go without figuring out who's responsible, the more people are starting to panic," Deacon said.

Recently, Deacon and his now wife, Leah, had gone through an ordeal with a copycat killer. Her co-worker, a detective with the Fort Worth PD, had become fixated on her after losing his child to illness and his wife divorcing him. He'd known enough about the case to cover up his killings by trying to make it look like the Jacobstown Hacker was attacking women on a jogging path in downtown Fort Worth. The path happened to be the same one that Leah had used every night at around the same time. The killer had been targeting her.

"With everything going on, the town's nervous. I get that. I'm planning to stay over at the McGregor house until things cool off for her. You think you can handle things on the ranch if I have to be away for a few days?" Nate realized he was needed but hoped for a couple of days to stay with the McGregors.

Deacon was quiet for longer than Nate was comfortable.

"She have a kid in Mrs. Eaton's class who just started a week or two ago?" Deacon asked.

"Yeah. I forgot all about the possibility of her being in class with Connor," Nate said. His mind hadn't been on the family lately. He'd been too busy being irritated with himself for falling down a trap with a woman so callous she could lie about her sister being ill. Maybe that was the connection he felt toward Chelsea? They'd both been lied to and deceived.

Granted, Nate had allowed it to happen. He should've kept his eyes open. The breakup with Mia had been his call, but he'd been trying to figure out how she'd outsmarted him for as long as she'd gotten away with it.

It hadn't taken that long to recognize her pattern. As soon as he'd figured her out, he'd given her walking papers. Nate figured the reason he'd allowed himself to think about settling down with one person was the happiness several of his brothers had found with their wives and kids.

But, hey, that kind of commitment wasn't for everyone. That was why he couldn't stop questioning his own judgment when it came to Chelsea. She was nothing like Mia. The two didn't even compare. Mia had been quick to try to lock Nate in while Chelsea seemed ready to put on her running shoes every time they bumped into each other in her small but cozy kitchen.

"Am I cutting out?" Deacon's voice came through loud and clear.

"No. Why? What did I miss?" Nate had no plans to share that he'd been lost in thought over Chelsea. Deacon would have a field day teasing him about that slip.

"I was saying that I can cover for you for a few

days. Wish I could offer more, but we're drowning right now and we need all the help we can get." Deacon paused. "I've heard good things about the little girl from Connor. He talks about the new girl and says she's quiet but nice."

Skylar had touched Nate's heart, too. Those big, round eyes, gap-toothed smile and curly locks could melt an iceberg. "Good to hear that she's making friends," he responded. "It's got to be hard to be the new kid in town."

"Yeah, we never had that growing up, but I saw it in Connor when he first came to live at the ranch." Deacon was in the process of adopting Leah's son even though Connor would always carry his real father's last name.

Connor's father had passed away from an incurable disease and, by all accounts, had been a decent man. Roger had died never knowing that his wife was pregnant because Leah had said she'd known it would break his heart. Roger had been abandoned by his father and had had a rough upbringing. By not telling him about his child, Leah had spared him the scars of feeling like he was abandoning his child. Roger never would have repeated the cycle of abandonment.

And that's why Deacon and Leah had agreed to keep Connor's last name the same even though he would have every right that came along with being a Kent heir. Connor's last name didn't matter. He was as much a Kent as any of them and no one would look at him any differently.

Nate had seen the way having a child had changed Deacon for the better. His brother was happy in ways Nate couldn't begin to explain. The same went for Mitch and Will. They'd found true happiness.

"Well, I've gotta get going, Nate. If you need any one of us we'll be right there for you," Deacon said.

"You know I appreciate it," Nate stated and he meant it. His brothers and sister having his back meant the world to him.

He and his brother exchanged goodbyes.

He thought about Chelsea and her mother. They'd done well without having much of a support network. Their love for each other was obvious. Linda was a hoot and she loved her daughter. There was something broken about her spirit, though. Nate figured there was a story behind it.

Zach wrapped up his call a minute later. "That Deacon who called you?"

"Yeah. How about your call?" Nate asked.

"Mine was from Patty. She's being flooded with calls after the fire with people wanting details. Everyone assumes the fire was arson and somehow connected to the heifers," Zach advised.

"Chelsea thinks she was hit before the fire started. That pretty much ensures it was arson, doesn't it?" Nate wasn't following the line of thinking about this crime being connected to the heifers.

"I'm with you. Captain Benton will probably rule arson." Zach lifted his hat and wiped sweat from this forehead with his arm sleeve. "Town's already in an uproar over the hooves."

"It's been a while, but someone who chops off a heifer's hoof isn't going to graduate to setting fires." The logic didn't work.

"You and I know that but try to tell Ray Royce that. Or Betty Orson. People worry and then that worry turns into panic. None of which will help us figure out who's behind any of this." Zach put his hat back on his head. "I have some calls to make."

A white van caught Nate's attention as it slowed in front of Chelsea's house. Nate and Zach exchanged glances.

A young-ish man popped out of the driver's side and opened the side door to the vehicle. He pulled out a large bouquet of flowers and balanced them on his arm while he pulled the door shut. When he turned toward them, Nate recognized the partially blocked face as Sammy Orr. Sammy was in the same grade as Amber, if Nate's memory served and he worked for the town's florist.

"Flowers?" Zach said almost under his breath. "Did Ms. McGregor mention dating anyone?"

"Not to me." Nate searched his memory. Nah, he'd know by now if she was seeing someone, wouldn't he? They'd shared one helluva hot kiss and he didn't make a habit of kissing a woman already in a relationship. He wouldn't think too highly of Chelsea if she'd allowed that to happen while she was seeing someone else, either.

Sammy stopped short of climbing the couple of stairs to the porch. "I have a delivery for Chelsea

McGregor. I'm guessing she's just moved in. Nice to see the Barstock house occupied for a change."

Nate took a proprietary step forward. The bouquet was massive. It almost completely blocked Sammy's face as he walked up. "Who sent them?"

"Someone by the name of Renaldo Vinchesa." The delivery driver shrugged. "Is Ms. McGregor home or can I leave these with one of you?"

"I'll take it," Nate said. The bouquet was filled with at least a dozen roses. There were other flowers that he recognized but couldn't name to save his life. The scent was sweet and romantic, and pretty much a slap in the face.

"There's a card in there," Sammy said.

Nate handed the bouquet to Zach and then fished out a ten to tip.

"Thanks," Sammy said with a quick smile and a wave.

Nate waved and clenched his back teeth.

The conversation he needed to have with Chelsea couldn't wait.

CHELSEA SAT ON the sofa in the living room, watching out the window. Rofert was asleep at her feet. There was so much comfort in having him around. She saw a delivery man hand off the biggest, most beautiful bouquet of flowers she'd ever seen. Her mind snapped in a couple of directions. None made sense.

Nate walked in the front door, his expression serious. He didn't seem any more amused than she was that the flowers had showed up. Oh. She realized why. He'd think they were from someone she'd dated in Houston. Maybe he thought she was still seeing him?

A piece of her was tickled that he seemed upset about them. Did he like her more than he was letting on? He'd kissed her and then kept his distance. She figured that he must've regretted it.

But the rest of her figured the flowers were from Travis.

"Who are those from?" she asked.

He set the bouquet on the coffee table and took a step back like it was a bomb about to explode. That shouldn't amuse her, either. It did.

"Renaldo Vinchesa."

"What?" Shock didn't begin to describe her reaction. The timing of these flowers struck her as odd, especially after his threats.

She pushed up to standing so she could walk around the bouquet to find the card. Nate must've realized what she was doing because he stepped forward and located the card for her.

The note inside read "Forgive a fool. Best of luck with your new venture."

He'd signed the card and she could vouch for his signature. She'd seen it many times on purchase orders for the restaurant back in Houston.

She blinked up at Nate as she returned to her seat, card in hand. "He's my old boss."

"Yeah, I remember." His feet were positioned in an athletic stance, his arms folded across his massive chest. He was in a defensive position, like he was fortifying himself for a physical blow.

"We had a purely professional relationship," she clarified.

"It's none of my business." Those words felt like a physical blow.

Based on his stoic expression, he didn't believe her.

Chapter Thirteen

"Don't you think it's a little odd that he threatened me when I left the restaurant and now sends flowers out of the blue after someone knocked me in the back of the head and then set my restaurant on fire?" Saying it out loud made it even more horrific to Chelsea.

Her restaurant was in ruins. All the progress she'd made so far was down the tube and she needed to start earning money soon.

Worse yet, she didn't have the funds to buy another fire pit to cook the pizza or the cabinets that had arrived and had been waiting to be put up. She hadn't bought insurance yet. An umbrella plan was unlikely but her best bet. Her only bet?

Nate moved to the couch and sat next to her.

While she had his ear, she continued, "I can show you the texts on my phone if you don't believe me."

The sound of tires on the gravel drive interrupted them. Nate was up in a heartbeat, checking out the window. "It's your mother."

Chelsea let out the breath she'd been holding. Her

pulse jacked through the roof at the slightest noise. Rofert stirred but Nate settled the huge dog down with a few words and a scratch behind his ears.

Chelsea bit back her second yawn in five minutes.

"I thought you were going to take a shower earlier." He eyed her up and down. "We can talk about your old boss after you get some rest. It was a long night."

"I was going to take a shower but…" She hated to admit the reason she hadn't done it already.

"Did something happen? A noise?" Nate's concern caused her heart to squeeze.

"I was scared to be alone in the house." She couldn't look him in the eyes while she felt so vulnerable.

He tilted her chin so she'd be forced to make eye contact. "You don't have to be afraid when I'm here. I'm not going to let anything happen to you."

The back door opened and her mother called out.

"In here, Mom," Chelsea said, the interruption breaking the moment between her and Nate.

"Hello, Nate," Linda said as she entered the room.

"Ma'am," Nate said.

"I better clean up." Chelsea pushed up to stand. She was weak and had to stop at the end of the couch to gain her balance.

"Take my arm." Nate wrapped one arm around her waist for support.

She held on to his muscled arm, wishing she could pull from his strength. He helped her up the stairs, one at a time, and to her bedroom. She welcomed the heat rushing through her body from the contact even though it was a bad idea to get used to it.

He turned his back, granting her privacy when she took off her clothes and put on her bathrobe. Luckily, that thing was so long it practically dragged the floor. She was keenly aware of just how naked she was underneath it when Nate stood next to her, helping her to the bathroom.

The past twelve hours had started taking a toll and exhaustion wore her to the bone.

"Will you wait upstairs?" Her fear was irrational, and she would find a way to get over it. For this moment, though, she needed to be around someone stronger than her.

"Yeah." His voice had that low gravelly pitch that sent sensual shivers skittering across her skin.

She closed the bathroom door and then leaned against it. The weight of last night's events hit her full-force and her knees threatened to buckle. Nothing could happen to her. Where would that leave her mother and Skylar?

Rather than get lost drowning in a vat of self-pity, Chelsea pushed off the door and started the water.

It was then she heard the floorboards creak and realized that Nate had waited for her. It was also then that she realized how much trouble she was in when it came to her feelings for him.

"I UPDATED ZACH on the situation with your former boss. He checked his notes and remembered you mentioning him on the first day he spoke to you," Nate said to Chelsea. She was fresh from the shower and had that clean, flowery, spring-like scent.

She sat next to him on the bed and her fragrance filled his senses, causing a reaction in places that didn't need stirring.

Nate needed to get a grip. He tried to convince himself that his reaction to her, naked and smelling like the first sunny day after a spring shower, was because he hadn't been out on a decent date since his relationship with Mia had ended.

But that wasn't entirely true. He hadn't been out seriously since Mia because no one had interested him and certainly never as much as Chelsea.

"Here." He lifted the covers. "Get into bed."

She shot him a look and he laughed.

"Don't worry. I don't go anywhere I'm not invited."

"That's not the problem," she said so low he almost didn't hear her as she climbed under the comforter.

He sat on the edge of the bed, feeling the same nerves as an inexperienced teenager.

"What is it about your mother's picture that made you have the reaction you did earlier?" He'd been curious about it, but the chance to ask hadn't presented itself.

Chelsea relaxed her shoulders a little, sat up and pulled the covers to just below her chin. She kept a piece of material in between the thumb and forefinger of her left hand.

She was a lefty? Curious. So was Nate. It surprised him that he hadn't noticed already. Especially since he'd noticed the right dimple on her cheek when she smiled. Then there was the freckle above her lip. Her soft skin and big eyes. He'd thought about all of those things more than he cared to admit.

"My father took that photo. My mother says he was creative and so talented." She shrugged but her eyes said the statement was anything but noncommittal.

"What happened to him?" Nate asked.

"That's the question of the hour. He literally went out for milk one day a couple of weeks before my second birthday and never came back. I don't think my mom was ever truly happy again." Her voice cracked a little, like the pain was still raw even after all these years.

"Sounds like a good reason to stay single," he quipped before thinking.

She frowned.

"I'm just saying I'd rather be single my whole life than suffer through a disappointment that punches a hole through someone's heart like that would." He realized in that moment that Chelsea had suffered through a similar fate.

Damn.

She shrugged again. "I guess. I've never experienced anything near that level. Not even when I was married. I cared about Travis, but I was young when we met and probably naïve. It didn't help that

I was so busy working my food truck business that I didn't go out much. I didn't really know what qualities to look for in a person. Guess I wasn't looking for anything substantial. Then I got pregnant. Turns out you can't take an antibiotic and expect the birth control pill to work."

She gave him a look that was equal parts adorable and frustrated.

"It still hurt like hell when he took off. The weird thing is, I don't think I was all that angry that he left. I was frustrated for Skylar. But I was more upset about losing everything I'd worked so hard to build. It never occurred to me that anyone could be so cruel. I look at people in a different light now," she admitted.

"Who wouldn't? Being deceived is a sucker punch. Especially if you care about the person who pulled one over on you. You don't have to be in love for that to hurt," he said.

"How would you know?" She bit back another yawn.

"That's a story for another time. Right now, I just want you to get some rest," he returned.

Chelsea had slid lower so she was lying down again.

Self-control was not normally a problem for Nate. But it was taking every ounce he had not to lie down next to her. She needed sleep. If she invited him into her bed, neither would get any rest. He could take the hit. She couldn't.

He started to get up but she grabbed his arm.

"Will you stay in here until I fall asleep?" she asked, releasing his arm.

"I'll do you one better. I'll stick around until you wake." There was a wing-backed chair in the corner of the room that he could get comfortable in.

He looked back at her in time to see her smile as she closed her eyes and released her grip on the blanket.

CHELSEA WOKE WITH a start, her lungs clawing for oxygen. A strong, masculine presence was by her side a second after she opened her eyes. It was dark in the room and she couldn't see anything.

"You're okay." Nate's voice soothed.

The mattress dipped beside her.

"What time is it?" She had no idea. She tried to sit up but her head hurt. She'd refused medication at the ER, wanting to have a clear mind.

"It's quarter to three in the morning." Nate used a flashlight app on his phone and set it beside her on the bed.

"What? I've been asleep that long?" Chelsea rubbed her eyes and glanced at the clock on the nightstand.

"Afraid so. Your mother has been taking care of Skylar."

"Have you been awake this whole time?" Didn't he sleep?

"I don't need a lot of sleep. Every once in a while, I stay in bed for a weekend and catch up," he said. "I didn't turn on the light just now because I don't want to wake your mother or Skylar. They've been through enough without causing more worry."

She gasped. "Did my daughter know you were in here?"

Skylar had rarely ever seen a man in the house unless something was in need of repair let alone witness one in her mother's bedroom. She would be traumatized.

"Yes," he said apologetically. "I told her that you had an accident while you were working the other night and I was making sure you were okay. She seemed fine with it, comforted."

When Travis had left, Chelsea had sworn her daughter wouldn't have men paraded in and out of her life. Once, Chelsea and her mother had stayed with a cousin of her mother's who'd had little kids and a different "uncle" sleeping over every few weeks. It had been confusing to Chelsea as a child and, as an adult, she saw it as inappropriate.

There was nothing wrong with a single mother having a sex life. Chelsea was beginning to want one of those herself. Especially with the feelings she was developing for Nate. But a parade of men through the house had always been out of the question. If her own mother had done one thing right, it was that.

"What is it? Did I do something wrong?" Concern had Nate's dark brows arching.

Chelsea needed to exhale and try to relax. "I'm sure one time won't damage Skylar's psyche. I hope."

"She saw that I was fully dressed," he said with

a smile that was a little too sexy. "And she asked if I could sleep over all the time."

Chelsea wasn't sure if that was better or worse.

"What about Mother?" she asked.

"Linda had pretty much the same response," he informed her. "She asked what I'd like to eat for breakfast."

Had everything she'd built up in her mind about being single and bringing a man home been paranoia?.

Given the circumstances, she decided not to put too much thought into it. There were so many other things to worry about instead, like the fact that someone at the very least had assaulted her and possibly wanted her dead.

"My head feels like an ex-thrower used it for target practice," she admitted.

Nate picked up a bottle of OTC pain medication along with a glass of water from her nightstand.

"I thought you might ask for these," he said. That smile from a few seconds ago played with the corners of his mouth.

She opened her hand and he dropped a pain reliever on it.

"More?" he asked.

"I'll start with one. I don't want to be completely out of it in case Skylar needs me," she said.

"Zach texted earlier and a waitress from the Last Bite Diner said Reggie's becoming quite the regular customer. He's showing up at odd hours, though," Nate reported.

"In that case, is he Zach's primary suspect?" she asked.

"He was until your old boss sent those flowers." She still hadn't showed him the texts. She reached for her purse and thought her head might split in two.

"What are you trying to get? Let me." He glanced around the room and must've realized before she could get the words out because he made a move for the dresser.

"My purse is over there. My cell should be inside." She pointed to her handbag.

Nate retrieved it and set it down on the bed. The mattress dipped underneath his weight.

She located her cell, which was out of battery. The charger was on her nightstand. She plugged in her phone and it came to life a few seconds later.

According to the icon on the bottom left-hand side of her phone, there were thirty-seven new texts. She pressed the icon and scanned through the few names. Several were from vendors. And then there was Renaldo's name. She'd almost deleted his contact info from her list but figured she didn't want to be caught off guard if he called. She wanted to know it was him, so she wouldn't accidentally answer.

Twenty-three of the messages were from Renaldo. She hadn't read many of them since she'd moved to Jacobstown, figuring his attempts to contact her would peter out eventually. There was no use fanning that flame by responding.

They'd been stacking up. The oldest ones sounded the most venomous. She tilted the phone so Nate could read them.

I'll ruin you.
You'll never work again.
You're a spoiled bitch.
Answer me!
You won't get away so easy.
You better watch out.
I could be anywhere.

"This guy was your boss?" he asked.

"Yeah, for the better part of the last three years," she stated.

"Were there no other kitchens that would hire you?" He read each text and the intensity of his gaze increased with each one.

"I'm afraid not. He's influential. I thought the chance to work with him was straight from heaven at first. My food truck was gone in the blink of an eye. The truck repossessed. I had debt. There weren't many jobs available where I lived at the time and I had to be close to home. Travis took the only car we had with him. My mom had her sedan and that's how I got Skylar home from the hospital. Mom had to run out and buy a new car seat because he took off with the only one I had. Money was tight. Then I heard about this job with a famous chef. Nice restaurant. I didn't have a lot of options even though I'd heard he had a reputation. I expected to get hit on, but everyone said he was so much worse with me. Like he developed a fixation because I wouldn't flirt back. It got worse from there. I was done with men and had zero interest."

"You couldn't quit?" He quirked a brow.

"My reputation wasn't the best after losing my truck. People thought I mismanaged the business. No one has the patience to listen to what really happened. I was good at what I did, but I didn't have real restaurant experience. Renaldo had a lot of influence in the Houston area and I didn't have the money to relocate. Not until now," she admitted.

Nate flexed and released his fist. "I can think of a few things I'd do to a man who takes advantage of someone in a weaker position."

"It didn't help that my self-esteem was pretty shot. I was so tired from caring for Skylar as a baby. Then there was my mom. I couldn't just walk out, and Renaldo seemed ready to make my life miserable as long as I stayed. I threatened to quit and he said he'd ruin me." Thinking about it now sent anger shooting through her. "He had influence and I didn't. If I went somewhere else, I'd need a reference. He made it clear that he wouldn't give me one." She pinched the bridge of her nose. "I felt pretty damn trapped until I heard from Aunt Maddie's lawyer. I had hope for the first time in four years. This restaurant *had* to open. It *had* to work. Now, I don't know what I'm going to do."

Hearing the words brought her to the brink of a breakdown.

"It'll be okay—"

"How? The restaurant is gone now." Panic welled inside her.

"We'll figure it out. I'm not going to let that be taken away from you, Chelsea. I have a feeling you're going to be very successful and I want to offer seed money," Nate said.

Odd that his words were so reassuring when there was no real reason to feel that way. There'd been a fire. She could've easily lost her life.

"You would do that?" Could she allow him to?

"Yes."

"Why?"

"Because you're a decent person who needs a break. I have enough money to help you get back on your feet as long as you're not too stubborn to accept it." His offer was tempting.

She had her daughter to think about and medical bills for her mother. "I can't afford to be stubborn, Nate. But you have to let me pay you back."

"We can handle the finances however you want to." His words came out final-sounding.

"I need to figure a few things out first on the financial end."

"Agreed."

A burst of hope swelled inside her chest.

"We need to show these texts to Zach." Nate motioned toward her phone and she figured he was changing the subject before she had a chance to rethink his offer. "He'll want to see this. He'll also want to drive to Houston and speak to Renaldo personally."

"Look at the more recent texts," she said.

I've been a jerk.
Forgive me.
Chelsea?
Answer please.
I'm sorry.

"That last one could cover several scenarios." Nate pointed out the fact that it had come in two hours after the fire.

"Right. He's a hothead and lost his temper daily. I'm wondering if he'd be so stupid as to text me threats and then set my restaurant on fire." She couldn't fathom it, but then his actions had left her scratching her head. Why fixate on her in the first place? Why would anyone want to be with someone who didn't want them back?

Chelsea had had plenty of time to ponder that question as a child. Even as young as twelve she knew her mother had stopped living, like she was waiting for her husband to show up and make everything okay again.

Life didn't always hand "okay" to people, not even to good people. In fact, pretty bad things happened to good people far too often.

"I've learned that people sometimes are that obvious with their words and actions. Only the most calculating ones don't get caught right away." Nate palmed her phone. "I'd still like a few minutes alone with him in a locked room. We'd see how tough he was then."

Nate was already taking screen shots of the texts. "I'm sending these to Zach so he'll have them first thing in the morning. He'll want to talk to this guy. The timing is weird, but Vinchesa doesn't sound like a career criminal who's used to covering his tracks. You'd be surprised at how many criminals give themselves away easily."

"What about the ones who don't?"

Chapter Fourteen

"Those can be scary as hell." Nate didn't want to think about the level to which someone might go to cover up deviant behavior. A smart person didn't get caught and that's exactly the type they were dealing with when it came to the heifers. Even with advanced security measures in place like installing cameras near Rushing Creek and adding security personnel and patrols, the responsible person hadn't been caught. All anyone knew so far was that the killer was male based on his shoe print. He was good at making certain that none of his DNA was ever found at a crime scene.

"Do you think Reggie's that smart?" It was a fair question.

"He's a known criminal. Someone with a long history of committing petty crimes could wise up with experience. Someone like him learns the system from the inside. Gets smarter every time he gets away with something." It was the closest anyone had been to so much as making an educated guess about who might be responsible for the heifers. But would the same man be stupid enough to try to hurt Chelsea? Would he draw attention to himself now? And why would the two crimes be connected?

The probability was low.

"Reggie seems guilty of something. He's been coming in and out of town undetected for the most part," she surmised.

"True. We have no idea how long this has been going on and the last time Zach had him in custody, the man wasn't speaking. He has a Louisiana license plate but Zach discovered the address on his vehicle registration didn't match his driver's license."

"There are no witnesses to the fire. Right?" Chelsea asked.

"No one besides you. We're still waiting on unofficial word from the fire marshal." Nate figured he could lean on the captain for an answer. The conversation would go over better in person, which was why he hadn't called yet.

Chelsea took another sip of water.

"I don't want to wake the house, but is there any chance I can slip downstairs and make coffee?" Nate hadn't had a cup in hours and he could use the caffeine boost to help him think more clearly.

"Depends on how quiet you are," she replied. "My mother sleeps like a rock once she falls asleep. But that can take a minute. Skylar fights sleep until it pulls her under. Once she's out, she's out. Rofert knows you, so I doubt he'll bark."

That was all the confirmation he needed. "You want a cup?"

"Is that a serious question?" She smiled and he liked the way it softened the worry lines on her face. The break in tension was a nice change. It was easy to talk to Chelsea.

"In that case, I'll be right back." He stopped at the door. "Are you hungry?"

"I think there's yogurt in the fridge. Do you mind bringing it up?"

"Not at all." He disappeared down the hallway without so much as a floorboard creak.

He flipped the light on in the kitchen and went about making the fresh brew. As he stood there with his palms on the counter, waiting for the machine to spit out the brown liquid, a thought occurred to him. Had the attacker chosen to strike at the restaurant because Rofert was at Chelsea's home?

Wouldn't that make more sense than someone trying to destroy her business for no reason? And he was damn sure there'd been an attack. He believed that she'd heard a male voice before she'd blacked out.

If it hadn't been for the winds, she might've succumbed to smoke inhalation. She'd gotten lucky. And what about the person who'd called in the blaze? Nate needed to ask Zach about the interview. Zach had surely investigated that angle by now. It wasn't uncommon for a criminal to call in his own crime, especially once he believed his victim was dead.

At the very least, someone was sending a message to Chelsea. He was saying that he could get

to her whenever he wanted. He could strike anywhere, any place.

Except home.

Rofert would've heard a noise if anyone had broken into the house. The locks were secure, too. Nate
had seen to it that the best locks had been used. The
windows had been replaced. Getting to Chelsea at
home would definitely require more skill.

Another consideration was that the attacker only
wanted to harm Chelsea. The person wanted to ensure no one else was hurt. That scenario pointed di-
rectly to her ex, Travis. Reggie wouldn't make that
distinction. He'd strike where he could and Nate
doubted the man would care about collateral damage.

Nate doubted anyone from town would have a
problem with Chelsea opening up a new restaurant.
People had been complaining about that building
being vacant for years. He'd only heard good things
from folks about her breathing life into it again.
There'd always be one or two complainers.

And then, there could be nothing to it. She
might've fallen and hit her head, knocking the heater
off the table and starting the blaze. Nate didn't think
Chelsea would lie. Her brain had been scrambled
in the fall and she might be recalling events out of
order.

He'd worked with enough head-injury patients
to realize Chelsea could be remembering wrong.

The coffeemaker sputtered and beeped, a welcome sound.

He filled two mugs, grabbed yogurt and a spoon, and then headed upstairs, stopping at the top long enough to set one of the mugs down so he could scratch Rofert behind the ears. Rofert seemed happy as a lark.

The old boy might have a tough time leaving the sweet family when this was all said and done.

NATE WOKE TO the scent of bacon the next morning. And a pair of familiar voices. Amber and Amy, his sister and cousin respectively.

A moment of panic had him to his feet and out the door in two seconds flat. The sun was up for now. The news had predicted a turn in weather. Nate hoped everything was okay at the ranch.

"Amber," he said from down the hallway. He'd heard Linda shout upstairs that she was taking Skylar to school a few hours ago. Nate had heard Linda return before letting himself nod off. All he needed was a couple of twenty-minute spurts and he was fine. He'd slept longer than that. He reminded himself not to get too comfortable in the single mother's home.

"Hey, Nate," Amber practically chirped. She met him at the door to the kitchen and gave him a warm hug.

Amy followed suit.

"What's going on?" He looked to Amy and then Amber.

"We heard about the fire and wanted to stop by

to see if there's anything we can do to help," Amber said. His baby sister and cousin had hearts of gold.

"Good morning, Nate," Linda said. "I sure appreciate you staying over last night to keep watch over my daughter."

"Much obliged, ma'am," he responded.

"How *is* Chelsea?" Amber asked.

"Physically, she's doing better. The high winds probably saved her from having more issues with her lungs," he stated.

"My brother told us what happened. That's so scary," Amy interjected. "I'm sorry she had to go through that. It sounds like she's very lucky."

Nate wouldn't disagree with that statement. But first, coffee.

He moved to the pot and pulled a mug from the cabinet. He didn't think much about his actions until he'd poured a cup, taken a sip and then turned around. Both Amber and Amy's jaws practically hit the floor.

It hadn't occurred to Nate how comfortable he'd become in the McGregor house and that must be the action widening his sibling and cousin's eyes.

"I see Rofert has been keeping you company, Linda." Nate redirected their focus. He didn't want to discuss his comfort level at Chelsea's house with anyone. Hell, he didn't want to put too much stock in it.

"He sits by the door until Skylar comes back," Linda responded.

"Aw," both women said at the same time.

"I shouldn't be surprised, though. He loves kids," Amber related, shooting an affectionate look toward the oversize pup curled up against the back door.

"I made bacon, in case you two woke," Linda stated. "I'll just go check on Chelsea."

That's when the women whirled on Nate.

"So what's *really* going on?" Amber asked.

"Nothing, I slept in a chair." He rolled his head around, trying to loosen the crick in his neck. "I have the knots to prove it."

Amber stared at him like he had two heads. "What are you talking about?"

"Last night. Isn't that what you were…" His blunder occurred to him midsentence. "*You're* asking about the fire."

He glanced from Amber to Amy. "I thought you spoke to your brother."

"We did. But you know Zach. He doesn't say a whole lot if he doesn't think we need to know. We've been hearing rumors about her distant cousin and something about a limp on his left side. Is that true?" Amy had always had a spunky side and Nate could see the twinkle in her eye.

"Yes, her cousin has a bad leg. Zach is checking into his background and whereabouts over the past couple of years," Nate told them.

"Is that the same person who set the fire last night?" Amber persisted.

"No one knows for sure. I haven't spoken to the captain about the fire yet."

"It's arson," Amy said emphatically.

"How do you know?" Nate took another sip of coffee. Dealing with Amy and Amber's energy before he had a solid cup in him was proving interesting. He didn't want to give away information that was inaccurate, but felt everyone should be in the know so they could look out for one another.

"I overheard my brother. He seemed certain," Amy said.

"Then the initial investigation is probably iron-clad." He'd tell Chelsea as soon as she woke. He'd witnessed the distress lines on her forehead earlier and hoped more information would help ease some of her worry.

Nate downed the rest of his coffee and turned to fix another. It was then he noticed the bags of groceries on the counter along with a stack of plastic containers filled with cooked food.

"Did you do all this?" he asked Amber.

"Me and Amy and the rest of the Kent clan. We all figured they could use a hand while Chelsea heals." The compassion in his sister's voice warmed his heart.

Footsteps sounded from the hallway. A fresh-faced Chelsea walked into the kitchen wearing a jogging suit. Her blond hair fell around her shoulders.

Nate's heart clenched.

"GOOD MORNING." CHELSEA'S gaze bounced from Amy to Amber. She saw the family resemblance and couldn't help but think the Kents had been blessed with amazing genes.

"We heard about what happened. I'm so sorry. I'm Amber, Nate's sister." She offered a handshake and Chelsea took it.

"I'm Amy, his cousin," the other one said. She shook Chelsea's hand next.

"Should you be standing up?" Amber asked.

"Rest does a lot of good, but I should probably take a seat at the kitchen table." There was no reason to push it.

"Coffee?" Nate asked. He'd been silently observing from the corner by the machine.

"Yes, please," Chelsea said, looking around. "My mother said you brought food. You really didn't have to—"

"It's nothing," Amber waved her hand like she was lazily swatting a fly. "The least we can do under the circumstances. We've been meaning to come by anyway and introduce ourselves. The ranch has been keeping us busy, but that's no excuse."

"This is too much." Chelsea choked back the emotion threatening to bring tears to her eyes. By and large, she was not a crier. Although she couldn't help but think a good cry might make her feel better if she could let out her emotions. Instead, she bottled them up inside until they threatened to choke her.

"We were helping your mother put groceries away when Nate came downstairs and we got distracted." Amy glanced at Nate before returning her gaze to Chelsea. "Is it okay if we finish what we started?"

Their kindness was a little overwhelming but

Chelsea was grateful. "I wish there was something I could do to help."

She started to rise, but Nate put a steaming coffee mug in front of her.

"Fair warning. Once these two get something in their heads, they go all-in." He smiled. Seeing that man in her kitchen first thing in the morning made her heart want things she knew better than to allow. Nate was intelligent, handsome and built like she couldn't believe. In short, he was dangerous.

"It's too much." Chelsea could lose her business and she would figure out how to get a job to pay bills. She could lose her house and she would figure out some way to find shelter. But she could not lose her heart. That was the one thing she wouldn't gamble.

Looking at Nate, she hoped like hell she wasn't too late.

"You guys are lucky to have one another." Chelsea's gaze moved from Amy to Amber, appreciating how the two moved in sync with each other. It was obvious they were close and seeing them made her realize just how opposite she must seem to Nate.

He came from a wealthy, tight-knit family. Chelsea and her mother were as close as they could be. They loved each other, but her mother had always held back, protected herself, even with her daughter.

Chelsea didn't blame Linda for guarding her heart. Or maybe it wasn't guarding at all. Maybe it was just broken and the pieces had never fit back together in the right way. There was no doubt her mother loved Chelsea. Loved Skylar. But once her heart had been shattered, she'd never seemed to recover.

It was the kind of all-consuming heartbreak Chelsea would experience with a man like Nate. And all the more reason to keep her distance.

MEETING NATE'S FAMILY a few days ago and seeing their generosity had Chelsea wishing her daughter could grow up surrounded by that kind of love.

Chelsea pushed the unproductive thought aside. She was doing okay as Skylar's mother. Wasn't she?

Nate had taken to sleeping in the guest room downstairs even though she'd insisted that she was well enough for him to go home.

Having Nate sleep at her house was a stark reminder of the danger she'd been in. She was *still* in danger as long as the person who'd clocked her from behind and then lit her restaurant on fire was still on the loose.

The fire marshal's initial ruling was arson, noting that the fire had been started from the inside. Any DNA evidence linking a perp to the crime had most likely been burned at the scene, so Zach was no closer to figuring out who was responsible.

Chelsea had contacted the estate lawyer, Michel Green, who'd relayed that the restaurant had been covered under an umbrella policy left by Aunt Maddie. Thankfully, Chelsea hadn't lost everything and she had a certain pride from not having to borrow from Nate even though she deeply appreciated his offer. There'd be a delay in opening—the fire set back her opening to the end of February at the earliest—and that was definitely more stressful.

Money would be tight, but Chelsea figured she might be able to eke by until then.

Nate walked into the kitchen where she sat at the table nursing a cup of coffee.

"I just heard from Zach," he said.

"What did he have to say?"

"You're not going to like this." Nate held up his phone. "Travis has been in jail for the past three years. He was locked up on illegal possession of a firearm."

Chapter Fifteen

Chelsea could scarcely believe her ears. Granted, Travis had gone down a dark path, but real jail time? For weapons?

And then another thought dawned on her.

"He won't be able to get custody of Skylar," she said to Nate in an almost whisper.

"A judge could grant supervised visitation, but that's the best he'll be able to get based on other cases I've heard about," Nate confirmed.

Travis was far more dangerous than she realized if he was involved in weapons charges.

"What if I'm not in the picture?" she asked. "What if I'm gone?"

"That would be tricky. Skylar has spent her entire life with you and your mother. If Travis had a real job and could prove that his home would be more fit…"

"He would never be a better option than my mother." They both knew that her mother's health could be made into an issue.

All this time she'd been afraid that Travis would

show up with court-ordered visitation or shared custody and he didn't have a leg to stand on with a judge. His threats the other day had been idle because he had to know it, too.

"I'm guessing that Zach has no idea where Travis is," she stated.

Nate shook his head.

Travis hadn't showed up since that evening at the restaurant as far as she knew. "He knew about the restaurant. I wonder how long he's been watching me."

"Good questions. Zach said he was released two months ago and has to see his parole officer on the second of every month," Nate advised.

"He must've just visited before he came to Jacobstown," she said.

"If he's responsible for the fire, he might skip his next appointment." Nate poured a cup of coffee and held up the pot. "You ready for more?"

Chelsea nodded.

He walked over and refilled her mug. He stopped for a second and looked her in the eyes. "He won't get to you or Skylar as long as I'm around. You know that. Right?"

"Yeah." The key was *as long as he was around.* He couldn't stick around forever. He had responsibilities on his family ranch. "At some point you need to go back to work. I feel bad enough that your family has sacrificed the extra set of hands this long. From everything I've read about running a ranch, it takes everyone in your family and then some."

"It's not the easiest way to make a living. It's a way of life. My family bought land a long time ago and got the associated mineral rights," he said. "We're fortunate and we know it. Our parents made sure we didn't take any of it for granted."

"I wish I could've met them. They sound amazing." She picked up her mug and rolled it in her hands. "I'm pretty sure I could benefit from a few pointers from them. I hope I'm not messing up being a parent too badly."

"You love your daughter more than anything else. Isn't that what kids need the most?" Nate had a point.

She wanted to give Skylar the world. But it wouldn't do any good if her daughter didn't feel loved. Chelsea loved her mother and the two had grown close over the years. She still remembered feeling like she wasn't enough to keep her mother happy. As an adult, she realized that her mother had been grieving losing her husband and the life she thought they'd have together. Chelsea came to realize that having her had probably kept her mother from completely falling apart.

Losing Travis in the way she had, facing the same fate as her mother, gave Chelsea even more resolve to make sure Skylar always knew she was loved. "I guess you're right. It's so easy to focus on my mistakes when it comes to parenting. It's this big, important job and I want to get it right."

Nate took the seat next to her and put his hand over hers. "I've been around a few babies recently and it's help me realize a few things. No parent is ever perfect. No kid is ever perfect. But honesty, forgiveness and genuine love go a long way toward a perfect relationship."

"Said like that, it makes perfect sense." Chelsea's heart pounded her ribs with him this close, touching her, but she managed a smile.

He leaned toward her.

Her mother's footsteps sounded in the hallway, heading for the kitchen.

Nate stood and grabbed his cup of coffee from the counter. "Morning, ma'am."

"You know you can call me Linda," she said.

"My apologies. It's old habit," he said.

Chelsea took a sip of coffee, enjoying the burn. She needed a reality check. Falling for Nate was out of the question.

"We'll go to Houston with Zach first thing tomorrow morning to interview Renaldo." Nate made sure Chelsea was settled in bed before he shut off the light.

"I need to be here with my mother and Skylar," Chelsea said.

"I'm not going without you. We have a pilot who can fly us down and back. You'll be home before supper." Nate had no plans to let Chelsea out of his sight until the case was solved. He wanted to be there when Zach interviewed Chelsea's former boss if for no other reason than to have Zach's back. He also planned to make sure someone watched her house to protect Skylar and Linda.

"In that case, I'd like to hear what he has to say." She pulled the covers up and settled in. "I'm guessing Zach couldn't pinpoint Renaldo's location based on the texts."

"No. So, he wants to interview him and get a feel for whether he's honest. We'll wait at a nearby café while Zach speaks to the suspect. That's as close as Zach will allow us to get." There were too many variables for Nate to feel comfortable. First, there was Reggie. Nate didn't like anything about that man. Everyone was keeping watch for him, though. And the benefit to that kind of scrutiny was that it would be much more difficult for him to show up unannounced.

Word had gotten out about Reggie's limp and that he'd been in and out of town doing who knew what.

Travis was more of an unknown quantity. He'd been in jail for three years and his first act after release was to hunt Chelsea down. Then again, he might've been keeping tabs on her from prison if he'd had access to a computer or friends on the outside. Controls were in place to prevent computers being used for devious reasons but convicts were cunning and could find ways around them.

Chelsea hadn't exactly been in hiding for the past four years. She'd been working and taking care of her family. Nate couldn't help but think someone as honest and hardworking as her deserved a break.

Life had thrown a lot at her, but she was still standing. He admired her courage.

At seven o'clock the next morning, the airplane waited on the tarmac. A checklist had been run through and Nate received the text that all systems were go.

It took an hour, give or take, to fly to Houston. They arrived at Renaldo's downtown apartment building by 8:53 a.m.

Nate couldn't help but notice that the modern building was extremely tall and that the glass had a blue tint that looked like it reflected the sky. There were sharp angles at the top. It was the kind of building Nate expected an entire apartment to be decorated in shades of gray: light gray walls with a dark gray sofa. The place would be all about the lines.

He couldn't imagine living in such a colorless environment but it suited some people. He was more of an outdoor campfire guy. A house with a fireplace and comfortable furniture was more his style. He liked being able to sink into a chair rather than perch on the edge of one like a bird.

There was a café across the street from the building by the name of Roasted Bean. It was the perfect spot for Nate and Chelsea to set up and wait for Zach.

The trio split up after confirming that Renaldo's vehicle was parked in the attached garage in the space assigned to apartment 1101.

Chelsea had been fidgeting in the airplane. She'd twisted her fingers together on the ride over and now she was tapping her toe on the concrete flooring while they waited in line to order coffee.

It was understandable.

She kept glancing across the street.

"You want to grab a table by the window while I order?" he asked, figuring she needed something to do besides stand there.

"Yeah, sure." She'd healed from her injury and the headaches had subsided. "He should be in there, right?"

"His vehicle is parked in its spot. There's a high probability he's in there." Plus, from what Nate knew about the restaurant business, a chef's world didn't get started until at least 3:00 p.m. and would run late into the night. An executive chef like Renaldo wouldn't likely arrive until 3:30 p.m. He would most likely have already been up and shopping at five o'clock this morning as the freshest produce and meats would be put out then.

Renaldo might be arrogant but he hadn't risen to his position in the restaurant business by being lazy.

By the time Nate got the drinks and sat, his cell buzzed. He checked the screen. It was Zach.

"No one's answering the door," Nate reported to Chelsea.

She groaned. "He might've gone back to sleep, in which case he'll be wearing ear plugs."

"I'll let Zach know," Nate said not wanting to ask how she knew the man's sleeping habits.

"Hold on. There he is." She pointed across the street. A man wearing expensive jogging pants and a T-shirt with bare feet came running from around the side of the building. "Security must've called up and warned him."

Nate bit out a curse and bolted out the door. He made a beeline for the shorter, medium-built guy with long hair and loose curls.

"Stop!" Nate shouted, hoping that Chelsea had stayed inside the restaurant and texted Zach. Nate should've told her to do just that but he hadn't wanted to risk Renaldo getting to his vehicle.

Renaldo wasn't nearly as fit as Nate.

Nate shot across the street and dove into the man, knocking him off balance.

"Where do you think you're going?" Nate said as he tackled Renaldo.

The chef screamed like he was in a horror movie being chased by a psycho with a chainsaw in his hands. The few people on the sidewalk cleared the way darn fast.

Nate landed on top of Renaldo, who skidded on the pavement.

There was no use throwing a punch. Nate used his heft to pin the man on the concrete.

"Freeze. Put your hands where I can see 'em," Zach commanded in that cop voice reserved for ordering criminals around.

Nate put his hands in the air and so did Renaldo. Of course, Nate kept his knee in the man's chest, which probably helped him be more compliant. If the jerk made a wrong move, he'd be picking his teeth out of the concrete as far as Nate was concerned.

"Let's take this inside," Zach said after a quick pat-down to ensure Renaldo wasn't carrying a weapon. "I'm guessing the security officer at the front desk told you I was heading upstairs."

Renaldo nodded.

The lobby of the apartment building had several chairs nestled together to the right of the main desk. The security guard shot an apology at Renaldo. No doubt his job depended on him alerting residents, but Nate figured Zach would have a few words for the man when all was said and done. Phrases like "obstruction of justice" came to mind. Although, to be fair, this guy most likely made the call as a heads-up and hadn't expected the chef to make a run for it.

Zach stood with his feet apart, hand resting on the butt of his gun as he instructed Renaldo to take a seat. Nate had seen the defensive position many times with his cousin while on a call. Civilians were allowed to ride-along with the sheriff. Nate had accompanied his cousin several times.

"Where were you last Tuesday?" Zach asked.

Nate's cell buzzed. He glanced up at Zach, who gave him a nod to indicate it was okay to leave.

The text was from Chelsea, as expected. He dashed across the street. Obviously, she wouldn't want to risk being seen or letting Renaldo know she was in the area. Being connected in any way wouldn't help, especially if he'd had nothing to do with the attack or fire.

"Are you all right?" she asked, worry lines etched across her forehead.

"Yeah," Nate said. "But the chef got a few scrapes and bruises out of it."

He was trying to cut through the tension with the joke but it fell flat. He could see how uncomfortable she was with her old boss nearby. Her toe was tapping again and she was sitting on the edge of her chair.

Nate took a seat. "Zach is interviewing Renaldo right now. If he had anything to do with the fire, Zach will figure it out."

"I almost want it to be him. Is that weird?" She blinked a couple of times before taking another sip of coffee. Caffeine was probably the last thing she needed but he acknowledged that it gave her something to do.

"No. You don't want Travis to be involved because that's unthinkable. No matter what else your relationship is with him, the fact remains that you're the mother of his child. As much as you don't like him personally, if he was sincere about wanting a relationship with Skylar, you'd figure it out," he concluded.

"Exactly."

"Because you love her. You have to keep in mind, he's never met her. He didn't hold her in his arms late at night like you did. He didn't rock her to sleep like you did." For all intents and purposes, Nate reasoned, the man was a stranger to his own kid. Another in a long list of reasons why Nate didn't much care for the guy. Mistakes, he understood. Dating the wrong person, he understood. He would never understand a man who could turn his back on his wife and child. That just wasn't in a Kent's DNA.

"You're right. I'm still trying to figure out what he wants with her and why he even showed up in the first place." She glanced left to right, scanning the coffee shop.

Yeah, the guy could show up and force his way into her life at any time. Chelsea seemed keenly aware of that fact. And she'd most likely be looking over her shoulder the rest of her life, wondering if Travis would be there when she turned around, given the way they'd left things after their exchange at her restaurant.

Knowing her ex had been behind bars for the past three years had to be yet another blow. Especially since he'd lied and said he was working. He probably hadn't wanted to show his hand to her because he'd wanted to threaten her with custody.

Again, what did Travis have to gain?

It was anyone's guess where the guy had disappeared to. Selfishly, Nate wanted Travis to be far away. As long as he was wishing, why not go all-in? Nate wished Travis would settle somewhere else, start fresh and leave Chelsea alone.

That scenario wasn't likely with a guy like Travis. Not if he smelled money. He'd cleaned her out once and Chelsea didn't strike Nate as the type to get taken a second time. It made sense as to why she was so guarded with him.

She'd been burned big time. And just like a

frightened or abused animal, it would take a boat-
load of patience to get her to trust anyone again.

Nate looked up in time to see Zach crossing the
street.

His cousin wore an intense expression as he
pushed open the door and walked inside the café.

"What happened?" Chelsea asked.

"He's guilty of something." Zach took a seat.

Chapter Sixteen

"Renaldo said he was with a friend at her place on the night in question." Zach's frustration was written across his features.

Nate had listened quietly as Zach recounted the story of the conversation between him and Renaldo.

"You don't believe him," Chelsea stated.

"He called her on the phone and I could tell she was scared to say anything against him. I need to talk to her face-to-face. See if she'll fold under the heat. You guys feel like taking a ride?" Zach asked.

"Did he mention the friend's name?" Maybe Chelsea had heard of her.

"Danielle French." Zach leaned forward.

"She works at the restaurant. She's a waitress," Chelsea said. "He goes through a variety of women and it does seem like he's with a different one every other week, but they weren't dating when I left the restaurant."

"The address he gave is not that far away." Zach held up his phone, revealing the map feature with an address on it.

"Let's go," Nate said.

They pulled into the Rancho Verde Apartment Homes' lot twenty minutes later. The place was on the outskirts of downtown, more in the suburbs. The structure was not as nice as Renaldo's upscale complex. This was more like a typical Texas apartment building. A front gate, which Zach got through by waiting for a car to exit, was supposed to keep loiterers away. It was easy to bypass.

There was a sprinkling of three-story buildings spread out across several acres. There were mini parking lots for each building and clusters of mail centers and laundry facilities.

The apartments were considerably less expensive, which wasn't a surprise given the pay difference between a near celebrity chef versus someone waiting tables.

Zach parked and exited the sedan. The way the buildings were set up, Chelsea stood behind Nate, using his heft to conceal most of her.

A female answered the door on the second knock, but Chelsea didn't recognize her voice.

"Ms. Danielle French?" Zach standing there in uniform would probably make anyone nervous, but this person's voice cracked when she tried to respond.

"No. I'm Cindy Staten, her roommate. Why are you looking for Danielle?" The words sounded rehearsed and a little forced.

Chelsea figured the roommate had been forewarned of this visit, just as Renaldo had been. Between his threatening texts and then his sudden change of heart with the flowers and apologies, she presumed he was trying to look as innocent as possible. Most innocent people wouldn't give it a thought. Whereas he was going out of his way to appear above suspicion.

"Is Ms. French home?" Zach asked.

"Yes. Hold on. I'll get her—"

Cindy returned a few seconds later with a woman presumed to be Danielle.

"Ms. Staten?"

She nodded, a skeptical look crossed her features. She was attractive. In her mid-twenties, she had blond hair and blue eyes, and was the kind of person who seemed to want everyone to like her. Chelsea also noted that Danielle was easily impressionable. She was exactly the kind of person an older man like Renaldo could manipulate. "Where were you last Tuesday night?" Zach pressed on.

"I was right here," Danielle supplied.

"Yes, she was here with her boyfriend," Cindy concurred. "Why? Did something happen?"

"Who is her boyfriend?" Zach ignored the question.

"He's her boss. His name is Renaldo," Cindy responded.

"And he was here?"

"Yes. Well, yeah…" Cindy paused as her voice trailing off.

"What does that mean?" Zach prompted.

"He wears really expensive, like, Italian leather

shoes and they were parked next to the front door all night. I didn't actually *see* either one of them. I came in late and left early the next morning. His shoes were here when I got home and were in the same place when I got up the next morning," she told him.

Chelsea figured questioning her was useless. The shoes could've been left there for days. The so-called girlfriend could be covering for Renaldo. Or maybe he'd threatened Danielle. Who knew? This felt like a dead end.

Chelsea's phone buzzed. She glanced at the screen and then showed it to Nate. The call was from her mother.

He took her hand and led her outside, away from the apartment, without so much as making a noise.

When Chelsea was clear of the building, she returned her mother's call.

"Everything okay?" Chelsea's pulse skyrocketed at the thought she was more than an hour's plane ride away and something could be wrong back home.

"I'm feeling light-headed," Linda said.

"Did you take your medicine?" Chelsea didn't mince words. This had happened before when her mother had forgotten to take one of her yellow pills.

"I think so," her mother said. "It's probably nothing, but I was wondering if you could pick up Skylar later. I'm going to fix myself a cup of tea and get to bed." Her mother coughed.

She could be coming down with something.

"Okay, Mom. Yeah, sure, I can pick up Skylar. Don't worry about it. Get some rest and I'll check on you when I get home before pickup." Chelsea started to end the call. "Mom?"

"Yes, honey."

"Are you sure you're okay? This is nothing I need to worry about. Right?" Her mother knew the difference between needing medical attention and having a virus. The problem was that she downplayed everything and Chelsea believed her mother didn't want to be the cause of concern for her daughter.

"I have Rofert here to keep me company and I'll be better once I get a cup of chamomile inside me. A nap will do a world of good. There's plenty of food in the fridge, so there's no need to cook. I ate some of the chicken and mushroom risotto the young ladies brought over. It was so good." Linda sounded tired but all right.

"That sounds delicious. I'll heat up a bowl when I get home for me, Skylar and Nate. Keep your phone on your nightstand in case you need to reach me. Then you won't have to get out of bed," Chelsea recommended.

"Will do, honey. Be careful on your way home from picking up Skylar. They said on the news the weather might turn," her mother said.

"Thanks, Mom." Chelsea ended the call and turned to Nate.

"I need to get home as soon as possible. Mother isn't feeling well and I don't like being so far away." Chelsea gripped her phone as she looked up to see Zach coming their way.

"Roger that." Nate, who had been fixated on his

phone, glanced up and locked eyes with his cousin. "What's the verdict?"

"Both of them lied but I can't prove a thing," Zach stated. "He's covering his tracks, but it could be that he's an overall jerk. He's in the middle of a divorce and probably figures he can't afford bad publicity. I don't like him."

"CHELSEA NEEDS TO get home. Her mother might be getting sick," Nate said to his cousin. He could see the worry behind Chelsea's eyes even though she did her best to maintain composure. She'd been uncomfortable ever since they'd landed and he'd picked up on her nerves. He didn't want to overthink why he was so attuned to her moods.

"I have everything I'm going to get from these people today. If I need to come back, it'll be with a local policeman and a warrant." Zach would need to inform Houston PD and get them involved should he find evidence against Renaldo.

"What did the girls say?" Nate was curious as they walked toward their rented vehicle.

"The two gave exactly the same story," Zach noted. "And that's why I'm not buying it. Usually in an interview people give two versions of the same story but these two sounded like parrots. Only people who have rehearsed a story beforehand use identical words and tell the story in the same way."

"I wonder why they'd cover for him," Nate said.

"We did pretty much anything Renaldo asked or we'd risk losing our jobs," Chelsea stated.

Nate flexed and released his fists, thinking that he should've gotten in a few shots before he'd let the chef stand up.

"Even lie to law enforcement?" Zach asked.

"He might be holding something over Danielle's head. I never gave him any leverage over me, but others did," she reflected.

"Like what?" Zach asked.

"A couple of wait staff got caught using drugs in the meat locker," she said. "Renaldo had them do all kinds of favors for him so he wouldn't report them."

"Does Renaldo use illegal drugs?" Nate asked.

"Not that I know of. He's high on himself as far as I could tell. That, and the feeling of dominating everyone around him." Renaldo had been a jerk and acted like a spoiled brat when he didn't get his way. "He liked to catch people doing things wrong. A cook had an affair with one of the married waitresses. Renaldo had a field day with that."

"And you? Did he try to catch you doing something wrong?" Nate asked.

"I never gave him anything to work with," she admitted. "All he could hold over my head was my job and my reputation. Both were important to me. The kitchen is all I've ever known and I'm damn good at it. I didn't want anyone to take that away from me."

"Were there sexual advances?" Zach asked as they made it back to the vehicle.

Chelsea had a good laugh over that question even though it wasn't funny to Nate. "Yes."

"And?"

"A lot of the waitresses gave in. I mean, he was considered good-looking. He has enough money to seem impressive to those without. He lives in a fancy downtown apartment and drives an expensive sports car. Most of the women he hit on were flattered."

The three of them climbed into their rented sedan. Nate took the driver's seat, Chelsea got in on the passenger side.

"What about you?" Nate started the engine of the rental as he glanced at Chelsea. "Did he manipulate you?"

"I didn't let him get away with anything," she stated.

"Where does he stand on your suspect list after speaking to him?" Nate asked Zach as he settled in the back seat.

"Right now he's at the bottom of a short list," Zach admitted.

And that left Travis and Reggie.

"Rumors are circulating that Reggie was heading up north. There was too much heat on him here."

"Can we rule him out?" Nate asked.

"Possibly."

THE FLIGHT HOME was quiet and bumpy. A weather system was coming. Chelsea worked her purse strap between her fingers for most of the time they were in the air. Zach studied his notebook or his phone. Nate acknowledged that he was getting behind on work at the ranch. And yet all he could think about was helping Chelsea get her restaurant off the ground.

The plan landed while he was still chewing on ideas. Chelsea was too proud to ask for help and he didn't want to overstep his bounds. But he did want to find a way to be of service. He'd figure out something. The number of bachelors in the family was dwindling fast. Especially since his cousin Zach had recently told him of his engagement and pending nuptials.

The thought of Chelsea struggling against her deadline to open the restaurant alone sat heavy on Nate's chest as he thanked Zach for flying to Houston to investigate Renaldo. Again, the thought of a man abusing his power by forcing people to do things they didn't want to do caused tension to cord Nate's muscles. If he kept thinking about it, he'd end up with a headache.

Chelsea rode with Nate while Zach took off in his cruiser, promising to get back to them as soon as he had news to report.

"I'm needed at the ranch before the weather system hits," Nate told her. He'd been keeping an eye on the reports. "We need all hands on deck to secure the animals in the barns before the front comes in. I'd like to take you to the ranch with me."

She shot him an apologetic look. "I should probably check on Mother and schedule a few contractors before I pick up Skylar."

Chelsea looked surprised that he didn't put up an argument.

"I'll do my best to get back before supper," he

said. He wasn't sure how long he'd be, considering his head had been out of the ranching business lately.

Nate pulled up next to Linda's car at Chelsea's house. He got out and walked her to the back door, linking their fingers.

The urge to kiss her had been building all morning.

"Before you go inside, I'd like your permission to kiss you again."

Chelsea turned around and locked gazes with him.

"You sure that's such a good idea?"

Chapter Seventeen

"It's a terrible idea," Nate said with one those devastating smiles of his.

Chelsea fisted Nate's shirt. She'd been thinking about the kiss they'd shared far too often. This was going to be the worst of bad ideas and yet she couldn't stop herself. Her gaze drifted up to his lips.

And then she looked into his eyes—another grave mistake—because the hunger she saw in them caused heat to swirl low in her belly. The feeling of a hundred butterflies releasing caused her stomach to drop.

Yeah, she was in deep trouble with Nate because this kiss was going to mean a lot more than she wanted it to.

She'd rather do emotional breezy with white-hot passion with him. The kind that burned intensely for a few hours before flaming itself out.

The fire between her and Nate spread.

Ignoring the fact that this heat could cause devastation like she'd never known, Chelsea pushed up to her tiptoes and pressed her lips against his.

His tongue delved into her mouth, causing more of that heat to rocket through her body. His mouth fused to hers. His breath quickened, matching the tempo of hers.

Chelsea had never experienced the kind of all-consuming passion that she did when she was with Nate. He was more than just ridiculously hot. He was intelligent and kind, which made for a potent combination. It was also impossible to resist for long.

His hands looped around her waist, pressing her body flush to his. His hands splayed against the small of her back and her stomach turned summersaults.

Every time she took in a breath, her breasts felt heavy and swollen with need, a need to be touched.

Desire built inside her and she was perplexed by how one kiss could stir up such a reaction in her body.

She pulled back long enough to ask, "Do you want to come inside?"

"Is that a real question?" Nate asked.

He linked their fingers after she unlocked the back door.

Once inside, he stopped her long enough to feather a kiss on her collarbone. She grabbed his hand and tugged him into the hallway where she stopped him midway to kiss him on the lips.

Their breath quickened as they moved to the stairwell. Anticipation building with each step toward her room, her bed.

The floor creaked and Chelsea froze. A few beats

later, she squeezed Nate's hand and led him to the top of the landing.

Her mother's door was closed and, after a quick peek, Chelsea realized the woman was sound asleep. Skylar was still in school.

Chelsea led Nate to her bedroom.

It didn't take but a second to close and lock the door. She turned to find him standing right there. He took her hands and lifted them until they pressed against the door above her head. He dipped his head and captured her lips. And her knees struggled to support her weight with the heat in the kiss.

His tongue dipped inside her mouth and warmth pooled between her thighs.

With her back against the door and Nate flush with her front, she thought about how amazing he would feel on top of her, crushing her into the mattress with his weight. She wanted to feel him inside her.

Her breathing quickened, matching the pitch of his as he toed off his boots and she stepped out of her tennis shoes.

Chelsea wiggled her hands free of his and dropped them to the hem of his shirt. He helped her by shrugging out of it and then she tossed it onto the floor. Hers joined his a moment later.

He groaned a deep guttural noise when he saw the teal lace of her bra. Then he palmed her breasts as she angled for her bra snap. A moment later, that joined the growing pile on the wood floor.

"You are perfection," he whispered in a low,

husky voice that sent trills of electricity shooting through her body.

She figured this wasn't the time to point out the stretch marks that he didn't seem to notice or care about as he dipped his head and captured a nipple in his lips.

Her body hummed with need as her fingers dropped to the waistband of his jeans. She fumbled with the buttons at first but his strong hands joined hers and he stepped out of the denim a second later. In his boxers, she could see his stiff length and another rocket of desire fired through her. Her mind tried to convince her that it had been too long since she'd had mind-blowing sex but her reaction was all Nate Kent.

He had buckets of sex appeal.

She dropped her hand to the erection tenting his boxers and his body stiffened with her touch. His gaze locked onto hers. There was so much hunger in his eyes, he made her feel like the sexiest woman on earth, flaws and all.

A few seconds later, she stepped out of her jeans. He hooked his fingers on either side of her hips and her panties joined the pile on the floor.

By the time they reached the bed, they were bare, naked, skin to skin.

The silky skin of his erection pressed against her belly. He looped his arms around her and kissed her so thoroughly her knees actually buckled. Strong arms kept her upright.

"You're beautiful," he whispered in that low, husky voice that trailed along her skin. "And smart."

He feathered a kiss along her collarbone.

"And sexy."

More kisses along the nape of her neck.

Chelsea pushed him back a step, causing him to sit on the edge of the bed. She joined him, wrapping her legs around his midsection, feeling the sexiest and most empowered she'd ever felt with a man.

It was Nate. He had that effect on her. She felt smart and beautiful and appreciated by him.

Chelsea wrapped her arms around his neck and tunneled her fingers into his hair as she kissed him.

She settled on top of his erection, slowing enough to allow the tip inside. She moved her hips until he was a little deeper inside. His tongue swirled in her mouth. And then her pace picked up.

She ground her hips and he groaned a sexy noise.

He brought his hands up to her breasts and rolled her nipples between his thumbs and forefingers as she slid on top of him until he reached deeper insider.

Bucking her hips, a well of need sprung as he matched her tempo.

Chelsea gripped his shoulders, digging her fingernails into his skin as he brought her to the brink of ecstasy.

Before she could jump off the cliff, he twisted her around until she was on her back, his weight pushing her deeper into the mattress. She loved the feel of him on top of her as he thrust his sex deeper inside her.

She matched his pitch as she felt his muscles tense. He was on the edge with her.

Faster. Harder. Deeper.

He drove himself inside her until her muscles clenched and released as she reached the peak of ecstasy.

He dove off the cliff with her, drawing out the last spasm.

And then he collapsed next to her, chest heaving.

By far, that was the best sex she'd ever had because it had felt like so much more.

"This changes things between us," he said so low she almost didn't hear him. "I'm falling for you."

Chelsea wasn't sure how to respond so she pretended not to hear him.

A few minutes later, Nate kissed her before getting dressed and walking out the door.

Why hadn't she said something to him?

Why couldn't she go there with him?

Why hadn't she stopped him from leaving?

A BRANCH SCRAPED against the window, startling Chelsea. The winds had picked up in the past hour and the cold front seemed to be moving in earlier than expected. She glanced at the time. She wasn't due to pick up Skylar for another half hour.

Rain droplets pelted the window behind her, making it sound like someone was tap dancing on the pane.

That couldn't be a good sign.

Rather than wait for the front to worsen, Chelsea decided to pick up her daughter early. *Better safe than sorry*, was her thought when it came to unpredictable Texas weather.

Brutal winds blasted her windshield and pea-size hail crashed against the hood. Debris blew around on the streets, which were empty, as most people were already hunkering down for the storm.

Chelsea realized half the kids had already been picked up by the time she got to the preschool. A moment of gratitude washed over her for not being the last one there.

Skylar ran to her mother and launched herself into the air. Chelsea put her arms out just in time to catch her. At close to forty pounds, Skylar was getting harder to hold.

"Momma!" the little girl exclaimed and Chelsea's heart nearly burst. Skylar had her father but a selfish part of her was grateful that she wouldn't have to deal with sharing custody. She was selfish enough to want every birthday, every Christmas, with her angel. Granted, if Travis had turned out to be the standup father Skylar deserved, Chelsea would figure out a way to make peace with being alone every other year for special holidays.

But Chelsea would be grateful for what she had.

"Are you ready to go, sweet girl?" Chelsea set Skylar down and bent to her level.

"Yes." That little girl's smile could melt even the worst day.

Skylar packed up her princess-themed backpack as Chelsea thanked Mrs. Eaton, her teacher.

Hand-in-hand, the two walked out of the pre-school. Wind pelted them the minute they stepped outside. Chelsea squeezed her daughter's hand a little tighter as she clutched her coat closed with her free hand.

"Ready to run?" she asked Skylar.

"Mommy? Who's that man?"

Chelsea looked up in time to see Travis in front of her pickup, leaning against the hood.

Her heart clutched as icy fingers gripped her spine.

"Can we talk about it later?" Chelsea had no plans to deliver the news he was Skylar's father.

She gripped her keys a little tighter. "Let's go home, okay?" she said to Skylar.

"Okay," came the response along with a giggle.

Chelsea hurried her daughter toward the pickup.

"We need to talk," Travis said as they approached.

"I'm sorry but I don't have anything to say to you." Chelsea she stalked past Travis, glaring at him. "Please stay away from me."

"We both know I won't," he declared.

"Do you care about me at all?" she asked, incredulous.

"Baby, I still love you," he stated.

Fire ants crawled across her skin as she opened the door and secured Skylar into her car seat.

Chelsea shut the door as Travis gripped her wrist.

"Ouch. You're hurting me," she said to him, forcing a smile to hide her reaction from her daughter who watched through the window.

"I saw you with that fireman." Travis seemed to grind out the words.

"Let go of me." Chelsea jerked her arm away from him, breaking his grip.

"You're my girl." Travis's voice sent a chill down her spine. In his twisted world, he believed those words.

"I belong to *me* and *my daughter*. None of which is your business, Travis," she stated as she stalked to the driver's side.

She grabbed the handle and opened the door just a little when it was jerked out of her hand and slammed shut.

Travis pushed her up against it and then his mouth was next to her ear. "Hear this. You are still my girl. That child in there belongs to me. And I have every intention of getting my family back."

Chelsea planted both hands on the vehicle and, using all her strength, pushed back.

Travis was caught off balance and stumbled backward a couple of steps. Chelsea rushed into the pickup and locked the door behind her. He banged against the window with his fist and she thought he might actually break the glass.

Skylar screamed.

"It's okay, sweetie. That man won't hurt us." Chelsea's heart squeezed at the thought of telling her daughter *that man* was her father.

This was not the man she'd known. Travis had

changed so much. Was it jail that had made him so cruel? Sure, he'd stolen from her, but he'd never wished her harm. This was different. *He* was different. And she was very afraid of what he'd become.

The engine cranked up and she squealed her tires out of the parking lot. Her hands shook as she reminded herself to take a few deep breaths.

The weather system had arrived, full force, as nickel-size pieces of hail pelted the windshield. Back at the preschool, she'd barely noticed the freezing rain while distracted by Travis.

Travis. Chelsea had racked her brain dozens of times in the past four years for missed signs. When she'd first told Travis she was pregnant, he hadn't been thrilled by the news but he'd come around. She'd been the one concerned because they hadn't been dating nearly long enough and he'd lost his job and had been down about it.

After being told about the baby, he'd accused her of having an affair and then walked out, disappearing for eighteen hours. His phone had been turned off. Chelsea, certain he'd leave her, convinced herself that she could have the baby on her own. Her business had started flourishing. It wouldn't have been easy but she'd been prepared.

And then he'd come back. He'd said that he'd needed a little time to think about being a father. He apologized for his initial reaction to the news and managed to convince her that he was excited about the baby. He'd kissed her belly and she'd wanted to believe him so much that she'd ignored all the signs that he wasn't telling the truth. The slight twitch at the corner of his mouth was his tell-tale giveaway.

Chelsea had ignored it. She'd wanted, no *needed*, to believe that Travis had wanted to be a good father. She couldn't allow herself to believe that her family history was repeating itself. She'd refused to think that she could be that naïve or stupid.

It had taken experience and hardship for Chelsea to realize that none of Travis's failures had been her fault. She hadn't been able to fix him any more than she could make him love his daughter.

The similarities to her family background had not been lost on her when Travis hadn't showed up at the hospital that early April morning—

An old Jeep roared up behind her, flashing its lights.

She checked her rearview and saw that Travis was behind the wheel. And then he tapped her back bumper.

Chelsea bit back a curse.

"Mommy, I'm scared," Skylar stated before crying.

If crying would help, Chelsea would have no problem doing the same. But she had to be strong for her daughter.

"It's okay. I get scared sometimes, too. Let's make this a game, okay?" Chelsea was searching her brain for something to say as she banked a last-minute right turn. But Travis followed.

"Close your eyes, cover them with your hands and count to one hundred as loud as you can," she said to Skylar. Her own heart rate climbed and she prayed the distraction would work. Anger burned through her. It was one thing to try to hurt her, but to bring harm to their daughter was unforgivable.

"One, two, three…" came from the back seat.

"Good, girl. Keep it going." Chelsea made another quick left-hand turn and then another. The roads were getting slick so she couldn't risk going too fast.

Another pair of quick turns yet the Jeep was still behind her.

Chelsea glanced around, unfamiliar with the surroundings as she continued to make left or right turns, trying to lose the Jeep.

This was not the time to realize she didn't know how to get to the sheriff's office from here. Her cell was on the floorboard, the contents of her purse being dumped out on the last turn.

She approached a bridge that warned of a lake and had no choice but to slow to a crawl. She wanted to turn around but couldn't manage it with Travis on her bumper. How on earth had they gotten to this place where her ex, the father of her child, was trying to harm her? Didn't he realize that his daughter could be hurt?

Chelsea white-knuckled the steering wheel, seeking an outlet for the rage building inside her. She had so much anger. She switched lanes and he followed, tapping her bumper again. He might be scaring her but there was no way she was going to let him win. Not this time.

The roads were bad. She wanted to gun the engine but couldn't risk the slick roads. Chelsea pushed slightly harder on the gas pedal and then switched lanes as Travis roared up to her back bumper.

What was he thinking?

Desperate, Chelsea scanned the road. Was there a turnoff? Would it be safer for her and Skylar if Chelsea pulled over?

Travis had to know that there was no way she was letting him get anywhere near Skylar. As far as Chelsea was concerned, the man would never meet his child after pulling this stunt. Her heart hurt for the fact that Skylar would never have a real father.

Of course, when she thought about an amazing man whom she'd prefer to have as her daughter's father, Nate Kent came to mind.

"Sixty-five, sixty-six…"

She heard Travis gun his engine, trying to slam into her on the bridge, but he'd only succeeded in spinning out. The Jeep banged against the guardrail. He must've hit the ice patch she'd managed to avoid.

Chelsea continued to creep along the bridge, her stress levels through the roof as her heart pounded her ribs.

She checked her rearview mirror but no Jeep came whirling up to the bumper. At least the heater in the pickup was solid, she thought distractedly.

Chelsea continued to drive but felt like she was crawling, looking for a good place to pull over. When nothing appeared, she took a risk and reached for her cell. She got it.

"Ninety-six…"

"New game, Skylar. Mommy wants you to take her phone and call 9-1-1."

"Is the bad man gone?" she asked.

"He is for now."

Chelsea knew the reprieve wouldn't last. With shaky hands, she handed over her cell.

She was almost across the bridge when a patch of ice caught her off guard and the pickup slid out of control before landing in a ditch.

Chapter Eighteen

"Everything all right?" Nate picked up on the controlled panic in Chelsea's voice over the phone.

"I told Skylar to call 9-1-1." Chelsea sounded confused as to why he was on the other end of the line.

"My phone rang and I answered it." It was all he could think to say. "Are you guys okay?"

"It's okay, Sky." Chelsea's voice sounded like she'd moved her mouth away from the phone. Then came, "I'm stuck in a ditch. The roads are slick and my tires spun out at the end of a long bridge over a lake. I don't know where I am exactly."

"Stay put. I'm on my way." He knew exactly where she was. He didn't want her to move an inch until he got there. It was also freezing outside. "Do you have enough gas to keep the engine running and the heater on?" Nate had already thrown on his coat and slipped into his boots. He was in his truck before she could answer.

"Yes. But there's a problem." Her voice was low, almost a whisper. "Travis."

"Where?" The answer was the only thing that mattered.

The temperature had dropped a solid twenty degrees outside. Hail littered the roads. Winds blasted the windshield. Conditions were worsening by the minute.

"I managed to get away from him a few minutes ago. He's on the other side of the bridge and he's probably trying to get to us." Again, her voice was barely above a whisper and he knew why. Skylar was within earshot.

"If we don't get out of here now, he might get to us," she said. Again she lowered her voice. "I'm scared, Nate."

"Is the road clear behind you?" He didn't want to ask outright if she could see Travis.

"I think so."

"Unless you see someone coming, I want you to stay right where you are. It's nineteen degrees outside and too cold for the little bean in the back seat." His truck was slipping and sliding already and he'd barely left ranch property. "The roads are going to slow me down. I'm a half hour away."

"I'm praying either you or Zach will get to us before Travis does." The line was quiet save for the hum of the truck engine. She dropped her tone to almost a whisper. "He was in a jealous rage and I barely got away from him."

The thought that Travis had said he wanted to be a family again with Chelsea and Skylar didn't sit right. As far as Nate was concerned, Travis had had his chance. Leaving Chelsea destitute with a newborn didn't qualify as a man worthy of a family. It would be one thing if Travis had straightened out his life and come back to her honestly. Nate would never stand in the way of a decent man trying to atone for past mistakes. Travis was doing the opposite.

Nate ran a mental checklist of anyone he might know who lived near the lake. There weren't many houses out there as of yet. A development was planned but construction wouldn't start until next year.

Best as he could recall there were two families who lived near Elm Fork Lake. Nate wasn't close to either of them. Was there anyone he could call who could get to her faster?

Nate's truck tires slid on an ice patch. He turned the steering wheel into the spin until the truck tires caught traction again. He realized calling anyone else wasn't an option. There was no way he'd put his family in danger. Each one would risk life and limb to help someone in crisis.

At least she'd called in the emergency to Zach. He or one of his deputies might be able to get to her in time. Nate feared he'd be too late.

"Someone's coming, Nate. I'm not sure if it's him." The panic in her voice sent a fire bolt of frustration swirling in Nate's gut. He needed to get her.

"Describe the area around you," he said.

"There's a clump of trees on this side of the bridge. Across the bridge is all lake." Her tone grew louder and her voice cracked.

There was one obvious place to hide that he knew about in that area. Too obvious? "Where's the vehicle?"

"Slowly making its way. It's still far but it won't be too long before it's here," she said, the sound of panic rising.

No one would willingly drive across an icy bridge unless it was the only way home or they were determined to follow someone else. That second option was a gut check and most likely the right one.

"Can you get across the street without the driver seeing you?" he asked.

"I doubt it," she responded.

Nickel-size hail pelted his windshield and this was just the beginning of the weather front about to batter the town. It was predicted to get a whole lot worse.

First, he needed to come up with a plan. It was clear that he wasn't going to get to Chelsea and her daughter before the driver of the vehicle on the bridge. Send them into the woods where they might lose cell coverage and they could get lost and end up freezing to death? Tell them to stay in the pickup and a jealous ex could get to them?

The fact that domestic abuse was a leading killer of women was not lost on Nate. He'd heard Zach talk about it too many times for it not to resonate.

"Doors are locked, right?"

"Yes." She paused. "He's halfway across the bridge. What should we do?"

Before he could answer, he heard the sweet sound of a siren.

"Can you hear that?" she asked. Her tone picked up, too.

"Help is on the way." Nate was halfway there and not nearly close enough. All it would take was one bullet to end Chelsea. Travis could disappear with his child over the border and both mother and child would be lost to Nate forever.

The thought hit him harder than expected.

Was he in love with Chelsea? He couldn't deny that he'd never felt this strongly about anyone else before. Skylar had his heart, too.

So, yeah, he was in love with Chelsea and he wanted to be a family. But did she? *Could* she open up and let herself love another man after what she'd been through? Mia's betrayal paled in comparison to what Travis had done to Chelsea and Nate wanted to shut it down for good. There was no doubt in his mind that Chelsea had feelings for him. The kind of chemistry they had was rare.

Even though it had only been a couple of weeks, it felt like he'd known her his entire life. It struck him as odd but he figured it had to do with being kindred spirits. Down deep, where it counted, the two of them knew each other. He'd known Mia for a year before they'd dated. Being around someone for a long period of time didn't always equate to knowing them. There was something honest and pure about Chelsea despite what she'd been through.

Nate respected her a helluva lot.

There was no way of knowing if Chelsea could open up to him, though. Being able to go there again with anyone was a whole different matter and only Chelsea could decide if she was up for the challenge.

"It's going to be all right," he said to a quiet Chelsea.

It was as though she was holding her breath, afraid to speak.

Nate pressed the pedal as hard as he could, pushing his speed to the brink of losing control. He *had* to get to Chelsea and Skylar. There was no other option.

The sound of Skylar's sweet little voice in the background singing the nursery rhyme that Chelsea had told her daughter to sing was a punch in the chest.

It was smart to distract the little nugget.

"There's an SUV with lights and sirens pulling up behind the Jeep," Chelsea informed him.

Nate's stress levels calmed with the news. He kept his voice the same timbre as before, just like he'd been trained to do in emergency situations. "Help is there. I'm probably ten minutes out."

He was making better time than he'd initially calculated.

The sound of a shot split the air.

The air was suddenly sucked out of the cab of Nate's truck. He bit out a swearword. "What happened, Chelsea?"

"It's the deputy who came over. Deputy Long. He walked up to the driver's side and then he was shot.

He leaned his hands on the vehicle and I thought everything was fine, but then he took a couple of steps back before he dropped to the ground. Nate, the Jeep is coming. What should I do?"

"Is Skylar out of her seat?" Nothing inside him wanted to give this advice.

"Yes."

"Get out of there. Run to the tree line and make a zigzag pattern. Don't just run straight. Turn a lot so you'll be hard to track and even harder to hit. Be as quiet as you can as you move through the woods." He paused at the sound of her pickup door creaking open and then slamming shut.

He heard rustling noises and what sounded like blasts of wind. Skylar's sweet voice was more of a whisper as she finished singing the song.

And then all he could hear was the sound of the wind.

"Chelsea…?"

No response came.

It was so cold that Chelsea's lungs hurt every time she took a breath. She cradled Skylar against her chest. At least her baby was warm with her face burrowed inside Chelsea's coat. She was grateful Travis hadn't come after her. He'd been busy wrestling with the deputy.

Chelsea pushed her burning legs as she hugged her daughter.

It was almost impossible to process the fact that a law-enforcement officer had been shot. Chelsea couldn't begin to allow that knowledge to sink in. Or that Travis was responsible. She couldn't fathom how wrong his life had turned for him to be capable of such an act.

It was crazy to think that her ex would go to such lengths to hurt her. She'd underestimated the potency of jealousy and anger mixed with desperation. When she really thought about it, Travis's life was over. Once he was caught, and she could only pray that would happen soon, he'd spend the rest of his life behind bars. All she could wonder was why.

Why track her down?

Why try to kill her?

Why ruin any chance he had for a future on his own?

Of course, at this point she had to consider his intention might be to kill her and take Skylar. He could easily slip across the border with their daughter as Chelsea had heard happened in custody cases far too many times.

For four years she'd wondered if he'd ever show up again. Unlike her mother, Chelsea hadn't looked for her husband. There hadn't seemed to be a point because there'd be no going back after what he'd done. But she'd always feared that he would show one day ready to take her daughter away.

Chelsea made a right turn, ran for a while and then made another. She'd been changing her course, just like Nate had said to do. Every once in a while she stopped to listen in case someone was calling for her, or worse, chasing after her.

The wind cut right through her coat.

Another right turn and this time she had to slow her pace for a minute to catch her breath. Running was one thing but carrying a little one while darting through trees, being slapped in the face with icy branches, wore her thin. At least hail wasn't a problem in the thicket. There were enough evergreens to keep a canopy overhead.

She'd managed to drop her cell phone before she'd reached the trees earlier. How long had she been running? Where was she?

She'd long ago lost feeling in her toes and feared frostbite might be setting in.

She'd wanted to give up more times than she could count but couldn't. Nothing inside her could surrender to Travis.

And then Chelsea heard her name. The strong, masculine voice trilled through her, bringing with it the first sense of hope since this whole ordeal had started.

"Nate," she said barely above a whisper.

"Mommy, I hear the fireman," Skylar said. "He can help us."

"That's right, sweetie." Chelsea spun toward the voice, drew up what little energy she had left and sprinted toward the sound.

She knew he was taking a risk in calling her name. He was not only letting her know where he was but was also giving away his location. Did that mean Travis was out of the picture? Had he taken off or, better yet, been arrested?

There was no way Chelsea was taking a chance.

She pushed forward, her toes feeling like needles were pressing into them with every step.

Another shot fired.

Chelsea froze.

"What's that noise, Momma?" Skylar asked.

She tried to speak but no words came. And, for a split second, the entire world stopped spinning. Time stopped. She was no longer cold. The wind stopped blowing and everything went perfectly still, eerily quiet.

A second later, as though someone flipped a switch, the world restarted.

"Nate," she whispered before taking off in the direction of the shot.

"Go back to the road," Nate shouted. "Run. He can't catch you."

Was Nate lying in a ditch somewhere? Bleeding out? How on earth was she supposed to leave him in the woods? He could be dying trying to save her. She'd never forgive herself if she didn't try to help him. But she wouldn't put her daughter at risk, either. The decision to run to her pickup or Nate warred inside her.

And then it occurred to her that he didn't *want* her to go to her pickup. That was too obvious and Nate was too smart to give away her location.

Chelsea spun around and ran toward the place where she'd heard the shot.

NATE CROUCHED LOW to the ground, listening for the sounds of Chelsea's footsteps over the blasts of wind. Travis had turned back to the road the minute Nate had yelled for her to go to the vehicle.

Travis must not've realized that his shot had gone wide and missed Nate, who'd been dramatic and played the part of victim. Thankfully, he must've pulled it off. Travis had retraced his steps. Deputy Long, who'd been shot but was alive, would be ready for Travis this time. Travis wouldn't catch the lawman off guard.

Leaving Deputy Long had been the most difficult thing that Nate had ever done. The deputy had been shot in the neck, but the bullet had missed a major artery. His bloodied uniform had made things look worse than they were. By the time Nate arrived, the deputy had already called for an ambulance and had insisted that he would be fine. He'd sent Nate into the woods to help Chelsea and Skylar. Long had promised that he would be ready if Nate was able to flush Travis out.

Time was running out. Nate needed to find Chelsea before she and Skylar froze to death. They'd been out in this weather for nearly an hour now. He scanned the woods as hail pelted his face in the clearing.

And then he spotted movement to his left. He eased behind the tree trunk in case Travis had figured out the ruse and circled back.

"Nate." Chelsea's voice was barely a whisper and the sweetest sound he'd heard in a long time.

His heart fisted as he popped to his feet and saw the look of exhaustion on her face.

Nate tore toward her, taking Skylar from her arms. The little girl was cold and Chelsea was shivering.

"Pull my coat off and put it on," he instructed Chelsea.

"You'll freeze," she said.

He could see by the determined look in her eyes that arguing would do no good. She wouldn't take his coat.

"Let's get you both to a heater." Nate knew the fastest way back to the pickup. It took fifteen minutes, which was five minutes too long in his book.

As soon as they broke from the trees, he saw his cousin's SUV. He took a risk running toward Zach but Skylar's teeth had started chattering. Nate bolted for the vehicle and was almost surprised when no shots were fired.

Zach, outside the vehicle, opened the passenger door and Chelsea immediately climbed in as Nate handed Skylar to her mother.

"Get them out of here," Nate said to Zach.

"You belong in the vehicle. I need to check on my deputy," Zach stated.

The door had barely closed before the first shot rang out.

"Please. Take care of them." Nate dropped to the ground and scrambled to his own vehicle. He knew his cousin wouldn't leave the scene when he had a deputy down. Zach would ensure Chelsea and Skylar's safety.

A ping sounded, a bullet whizzed past Nate's ear.

Damn. That was a little too close for comfort. He dove, rolled and then popped to his feet behind his truck. He could climb in the cab, but then what?

Nate palmed his handgun.

He slowly looked around the side of his vehicle. Another shot was fired. He drew out two more as Nate counted shots.

Travis's gun was empty.

The man could reload, if he had more ammunition, and that would take a minute or two. Nate seized the opportunity and bolted for the area from where the shots had been fired.

The shooter looked up and Nate immediately recognized Travis Zucker from the photo Zach had once showed him. The panicked look on the man's face said he knew he was outmatched. Adrenaline must've kicked in because his hands shook as he tried to reload. That played to Nate's advantage because bullets dropped to the ground.

Nate got his own burst of energy, so he propelled himself at Travis.

The guy was small but quick, rolling out of the way at the last second.

Nate tried to adjust midair but collided with the hard ground. Bullets littered the cold, unforgiving earth as he scrambled to his knees and jerked right. Travis was trying to flee.

Nate managed to grab an ankle. Travis used the butt of his rifle to slam Nate's hand, trying to use the weapon to force Nate to let go. It landed on his index finger and hurt like hell. Travis kicked but Nate's grip was steely. There was no way in hell Travis was getting away when Nate had the man this close.

He took another jab, this time to his wrist, and feared it might've fractured. Pain shot up his arm and his fingers went completely numb. Sheer force of will caused Nate to dig his fingers into the skin of Travis's ankle deeper.

"Get. Off. Me." The words came out through labored breaths.

"Give up, Travis. You're going to jail. Why make it worse?" Nate growled as he pulled his left hand up to grab the man's calf.

"Not. Happening." Travis slammed the butt of the gun into Nate's skull.

His vision blurred and pain shot down his neck, but he had the presence of mind to grab hold of the weapon. Now he and Travis were in a dangerous game of tug-of-war.

Nate doubled down and let go of Travis's ankle. It didn't take long to yank the rifle out of Travis's hands but he stomped on Nate's head.

Nate had had enough. Rising, he threw the rifle as far as he could, knowing full well where it landed.

And then he grabbed Travis, first by the wrist as a fist flew at Nate.

Nate brought his knee up at the same time he jerked Travis's arm down. When knee met face, Travis screamed in pain.

Capitalizing on the moment, Nate threw Travis to the ground face-first and thrust his knee into the man's back to pin him down. He grabbed Travis by the wrists and yanked his arms behind his back.

Nate's cell was long lost, so he shouted for help. He didn't have any wire or cable with him to tie Travis up. Hell, he'd leave the man tied to a tree and let hungry coyotes and cougars do the rest if it were up to him.

But then death would be too easy a way out for Travis. And there was always that rare chance the man might figure out an escape.

Travis needed to suffer. He needed to see what real justice looked like. Living the rest of his life behind bars for attempted murder, attempted capital murder and a host of other offenses, including domestic abuse and violence would teach him a thing or two about how to treat other people, especially someone who'd cared about him at one time.

Nate shouted for help again. His wrists hurt like hell and he was developing a massive headache. Thankfully, the cold was probably keeping his wrist from swelling.

He listened for a response but got none.

If he spent much more time outside, he'd freeze. Nate needed to get Travis to the road.

"We're going for a walk." Nate took off his belt with a yank and used it to bind Travis's hands together.

And then Nate forced the man to stand and walk toward his reckoning.

Chapter Nineteen

"Get down. Face down," Nate demanded as soon as he walked Travis back to the pickup.

"I can't. My hands," Travis complained.

Nate found it interesting the man could be a bully with someone smaller than him. With Nate, he was just a complaining punk. Of course, give the man an opportunity and he wouldn't hesitate to capitalize on it. Cowards usually hid behind weapons.

"On your knees or I'll help you," Nate said. "Don't test me."

Awkwardly, Travis complied.

Nate gripped the back of the man's neck and pushed him to the ground behind his pickup.

Travis grumbled some kind of complaint or threat that Nate couldn't make out. He didn't care, either.

In the rear of his truck, he located cable wire. He used that to bind Travis's hands behind his back.

"What are you, a cop?" Travis asked.

"You wish. I have no rules keeping me from beating you until you drop," Nate retorted as he tightened the bindings.

"Ouch. That hurts, man. Don't be a jerk," Travis said.

Nate didn't bother to respond. He texted his cousin that Travis was in his custody and it was safe to come back to pick the scumbag up.

"Tell me one thing…" Nate said to Travis.

"Why should I?" Travis shot back.

Nate shrugged. "Be a man just this one time and tell me why you tried to burn down her restaurant."

"Who said I did?" Travis countered.

Nate picked Travis up by his wrists.

Travis released a string of swearwords as he winced in pain.

"Why?" was all Nate asked.

Travis looked up at Nate. "Because she didn't want me."

"So you tried to kill her?" Nate asked.

"Scare. I only meant to scare her just like when I threw the rock in her window," Travis admitted. A look of anguish crossed his features. "Thought it might make her want to give me another chance."

"She could've died, you idiot." Nate could hardly believe the man thought she'd want to be in the same room with him.

"Yeah, well, I got in over my head. I was blinded and figured if I couldn't have her no one should." There was a dead quality to Travis's eyes now. Nate had seen it before in men who'd crossed a line they could never come back from.

"You almost made your daughter an orphan. That's not just stupid and cruel, it's criminal." Nate had no sympathy for the man. He figured Chelsea would appreciate knowing that Travis hadn't actually been trying to kill her. He was sick and twisted, but he hadn't wanted her dead.

"I never did truly believe that kid was mine," Travis stated. "I would've claimed her anyhow."

Shock didn't begin to describe the blow Nate took on that one.

"Really? Why not?" Zach's SUV was a dot in the distance, growing bigger.

"She was on birth control and there was a guy she worked for that kept flirting with her."

Was he kidding?

"Did you think to get a DNA test?" Nate asked, incredulous, though it explained why the man had ruined her business and abandoned their child.

Travis stood there, anger scoring his forehead as Zach made a beeline toward them.

"You're going away for a long time, Travis."

CHELSEA'S HEART SQUEEZED when she saw Nate. The thought of anything happening to him had nearly broken her in two.

An ambulance had arrived and loaded Deputy Long inside. The EMT gave a thumbs-up sign to Zach, who said that meant his deputy was going to be fine.

"Momma, it's the fireman," Skylar said, pointing to Nate.

"Yes, it is," Chelsea said, fighting tears of relief.

"I'm hungry. Is it dinnertime yet?" Skylar asked.

Chelsea couldn't help but smile at her daughter. Kids had a unique ability to live in the moment. That was most likely why they were so happy. Ten minutes after a stressful event, they moved on. Especially if a toy was thrown into the mix.

Zach forced Travis to spread eagle, his chest against the hood of Deputy Long's SUV, before handcuffing him.

Nate walked toward Chelsea and her heart pounded her ribs.

"Momma, the fireman's coming here." Skylar clapped. Thankfully, they were warm inside the SUV thanks to Nate. If he hadn't showed up when he had, she and Skylar might still be wandering around in those woods. Chelsea shuddered thinking about what might've happened. She didn't care so much about what happened to her but thinking something might've happened to her daughter…

She couldn't even go there hypothetically.

"I know, sweetheart." Chelsea tried to mask her over-the-top reaction.

"I like him," Skylar stated with all the pomp and circumstance of a four-year-old.

"I do, too," Chelsea said softly. She hadn't been certain that she could allow herself to really fall for someone again. But there she was head-over-heels for Nate Kent. And now that this big mystery was solved, he'd go right back to his life and she'd go to hers. Why did that suddenly sound so empty?

Nate opened the driver's side door of his truck as

Skylar climbed in back. Chelsea she scooted over so he could slide in beside her.

"You're freezing," she said to him as he rubbed his hands together before blowing on them.

Nate leaned toward her and gave her a quick kiss.

"What did you think about being in a cruiser?" he asked Skylar, who was beaming at him.

"The policeman let me push a button to turn on the lights," she said proudly.

Yeah, Chelsea was in trouble, all right. She had feelings for Nate, feelings that wouldn't go away easily. Her daughter had taken to him the first time they'd met.

A weight pressed on Chelsea's limbs.

"You should stop by and check out the fire truck someday. We have so many more lights to play with," he said.

Skylar's face lit up.

"You want a ride home?" he asked Chelsea. "We'll get your pickup towed once the cold front blows over tomorrow afternoon."

"That would be great," she said.

"I'll get Skylar's car seat." Nate hopped out of the vehicle before she could stop him. She had no idea what she was going to say to him. She just didn't want him to leave.

THE RIDE HOME was quiet. Zach was transporting Travis to jail where he'd be locked up a very long time. Chelsea felt safe. Skylar sang in the back seat and played with the baby doll Nate had brought over from the ditched pickup. Chelsea and Nate sat in companionable silence.

At home, Chelsea checked on her mother then ate dinner with Skylar and Nate.

She put her daughter to bed, grateful that he'd waited around. He was standing in her kitchen, pouring two mugs of coffee, looking like the sexy man that he was.

"Thanks for hanging around tonight," Chelsea said to him as he handed a fresh mug to her.

He didn't respond and she figured he was choosing his words carefully. He'd been nothing but considerate and she assumed he'd let her down easy.

"I spoke to Travis…" Nate started to say.

"What did he have to say?" She rolled the warm mug in the palms of her hands.

"That he thought you were having an affair with one of your employees." There was no suspicion in his eyes and she appreciated him for it. Thinking back, Travis had become a little fixated on her friendship with Collier Stead.

"He brought it up a couple of times before he disappeared, but I couldn't believe he'd think that," she said.

"He doesn't know you very well, does he?"

"Not if he seriously believed I'd cheat." She stared at Nate. "How do you know that I didn't?"

"You're one of kindest and most honest people I've ever met. You're loyal to a fault. You wouldn't have an affair." His certainty caused warmth to rocket through her. "You're also beautiful, but that's a whole other conversation."

Her cheeks flamed.

Being with Nate made her feel beautiful.

"How do you know all this when I've only known you for a short time?" she asked. He was spot-on, though. She'd never cheat.

"I've felt a connection with you like I've never felt before, Chelsea. I know you've been through a lot with men, and it might be hard to trust, but I know you. And I think you know me, too," he stated.

"If anyone had told me that I could fall for someone this hard, this fast, and it would turn out to be real, I wouldn't believe them." It was true. "I feel like I know you from somewhere down deep. Is that weird?"

"I feel it, too," he said. "But you have a lot on your plate. You're building a restaurant almost from the ground up. You have a daughter who needs you every day, not to mention your mother."

This was the part where he let her down easy. And it was suddenly hard to breathe.

"That's all true," she confirmed.

"I might be throwing you a curveball…" He walked to her and dropped down on one knee. "That's why I think we shouldn't wait to get married."

"What?" She was pretty certain she hadn't heard him correctly.

"We can go through the motions of dating, steal time here and there, but I love you and I want you to be my wife. I want you and Skylar to be my family.

Forever. And I don't see a good reason to wait. But if you do, I understand. I'm ready to do whatever it takes and if that means waiting, going slow, I will. I want to be in your life any way you'll allow. I'm patient and I can hold off until you're ready to trust me one hundred percent with your heart."

Chelsea's heart leaped for joy. Life had gotten really good at throwing curveballs at her. Finally, it tossed her one she wanted to catch and hold onto.

"I love you, too, Nate." She did. She loved him with her whole heart. "I can't think of one reason to wait to be your wife."

"Is that a yes?" A wide smile broke across that beautiful face of his.

"Yes." She set her coffee mug down as he stood. She wrapped her arms around his neck. "I will marry you."

Nate kissed her so hard it robbed her breath.

He pulled back and pressed his forehead against hers. "I've been waiting for you my whole life," he said. "Linda felt like family from the first time we met. With you and Skylar, I've found home."

Home.

Chelsea couldn't think of a better word to describe the way she felt about Nate.

And she finally had a real place to call home.

* * * * *

Look for the next book in USA TODAY
bestselling author Barb Han's
Rushing Creek Crime Spree miniseries,
What She Knew,
available next month.

And don't miss the previous books in the series:

Cornered at Christmas
Ransom at Christmas
Ambushed at Christmas

Available now from Harlequin Intrigue!

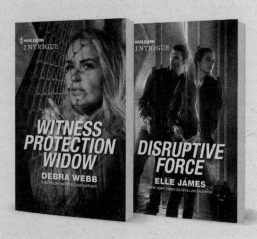

COMING NEXT MONTH FROM

H HARLEQUIN

INTRIGUE

Available April 21, 2020

#1923 SECRET INVESTIGATION
Tactical Crime Division • by Elizabeth Heiter
When battle armor inexplicably fails and soldiers perish, the Tactical Crime Division springs into action. With the help of Petrov Armor CEO Leila Petrov, can undercover agent Davis Rogers discover secrets larger than anyone ever imagined?

#1924 CONARD COUNTY JUSTICE
Conard County: The Next Generation • by Rachel Lee
Major Daniel Duke will do whatever it takes to catch his brother's killer, but Deputy Cat Jansen is worried that he'll hinder her investigation. As the stakes increase, they must learn to work together to find the murderer. If they can't, they could pay with their lives...

#1925 WHAT SHE KNEW
Rushing Creek Crime Spree • by Barb Han
When a baby appears on navy SEAL Rylan Anderson's doorstep, he enlists old friend Amber Kent for help. But when the child is nearly abducted in Amber's care, they realize they must discover the truth behind the baby's identity in order to stop the people trying to kidnap her.

#1926 BACKCOUNTRY ESCAPE
A Badlands Cops Novel • by Nicole Helm
Felicity Harrison is being framed for murder. Family friend Gage Wyatt vows to keep her safe until they find the real culprit, but there's a killer out there who doesn't just want Felicity framed—but silenced for good.

#1927 THE HUNTING SEASON
by Janice Kay Johnson
After a string of murders connected to CPS social worker Lindsay Eagle's caseload is discovered, Detective Daniel Deperro is placed on protective detail. But Lindsay won't back down from the investigation, even as Daniel fears she's the next target. Will his twenty-four-hour protection enrage the killer further?

#1928 MURDER IN THE SHALLOWS
by Debbie Herbert
When a routine patrol sets Bailey Covington on the trail of a serial killer, the reclusive park ranger joins forces with sheriff's deputy Dylan Armstrong. Bailey can't forgive Dylan's family for betraying her, but they'll have to trust each other to find two missing women before a murderer strikes again.

YOU CAN FIND MORE INFORMATION ON UPCOMING HARLEQUIN TITLES, FREE EXCERPTS AND MORE AT HARLEQUIN.COM.

HICNM0420

She wiped up stray crumbs, then tried to smile at him. "Coffee?"

"I've intruded too much."

She put a hand on her hip. "I might have thought so earlier, but I'm not feeling that way now. This is important. I give a damn about Larry, and now I give a damn about you. You might not want it, but I care. So quiet down. Coffee? Or something else?"

"A beer if you have another."

As it happened, she did. "I buy this so rarely that you're in luck."

"Then why did you buy it?"

"Larry," she answered simply.

For the first time, they shared a look of real understanding. The sense of connection warmed her.

HIEXP0420

She hadn't expected to feel this way, not when it came to Duke. Maybe it helped to realize he wasn't just a monolith of anger and unswaying determination.

As Cat returned to her seat, she said, "You put me off initially."

Another half smile from him. "I never would have guessed."

A laugh escaped her, brief but genuine. "I'm usually better at concealing my reactions to people. But there you were, looking like a battering ram. You sure looked hard and angry. Nothing about you made me want to get into a tussle."

He looked at the beer bottle he held. "Most people don't want to tangle with me. I can understand your reaction. I came through that door loaded for bear. Too much time to think on the way here, maybe."

"You looked like walking death," she told him frankly. "An icy-cold fury. Worse, in my opinion, than a heated rage. Scary."

"Comes with the territory," he said after a moment, then took a swig of his beer.

She could probably wonder until the cows came home exactly what he meant by that. Maybe it was better not to know.

Don't miss
Conard County Justice *by Rachel Lee,*
available May 2020 wherever
Harlequin Intrigue books and ebooks are sold.

Harlequin.com

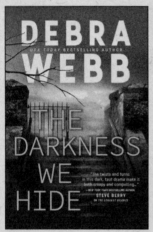

SPECIAL EXCERPT FROM

mira

*Dr. Rowan Dupont and police chief Billy Brannigan
have one final opportunity to catch dangerous serial
killer Julian Addington, but will their teamwork be
enough to stop him—or will he find them first?*

Read on for a sneak preview of
The Darkness We Hide
by USA TODAY *bestselling author Debra Webb.*

*Winchester, Tennessee
Monday, March 9, 7:35 a.m.*

Rowan Dupont parked on the southeast side of the downtown square. The county courthouse sat smack in the middle of Winchester with streets forming a grid around it. Shops, including a vintage movie theater, revitalized over the past few years by local artisans, lined the sidewalks. Something Rowan loved most about her hometown were the beautiful old trees that still stood above all else. So often the trees were the first things to go when towns received a face-lift. Not in Winchester. The entire square had been refreshed and the majestic old trees still stood.

This morning the promise of spring was impossible to miss. Blooms and leaves sprouted from every bare limb. This was her favorite time of year. A new beginning. Anything could happen.

Rowan sighed. Funny how being back in Winchester had come to mean so much to her these past several months. As a teenager she couldn't wait to get away from home. Growing up in a funeral home had made her different from the other kids. She was the daughter of the undertaker, a curiosity. At twelve tragedy had struck and she'd lost her twin sister and her mother within months of each other. The painful events had driven her to the very edge. By the time she'd finished high school, she was beyond ready for a change of scenery. Despite having spent more than twenty years living in the big city hiding from the memories of home and a dozen of those two decades working with Nashville's police department—in Homicide, no less—she had been forced to see that there was no running away. No hiding from the secrets of her past.

There were too many secrets, too many lies, to be ignored.

Yet despite all that had happened the first eighteen years of her life, she was immensely glad to be back home.

If only the most painful part of her time in Nashville— serial killer Julian Addington—hadn't followed her home and wreaked havoc those first months after her return.

Rowan took a breath and emerged from her SUV. The morning air was brisk and fresh. More glimpses of spring's impending arrival showed in pots overflowing with tulips, daffodils and crocuses. Those same early bloomers dotted the landscape beds all around the square. It was a new year and she was very grateful to have the previous year behind her.

She might not be able to change the past, but she could forge a different future, and she intended to do exactly that.

Don't miss
The Darkness We Hide *by Debra Webb,*
available April 2020 wherever
MIRA books and ebooks are sold.

Harlequin.com